Sophie Cunningham is Australian and has worked in publishing for fifteen years as an editor of fiction and non-fiction, and as a publisher. She is the television columnist for *The Age* in Melbourne. *Geography* is her first novel.

www.**booksattransworld**.co.uk

Geography

Sophie Cunningham

BLACK SWAN

GEOGRAPHY
A BLACK SWAN BOOK : 0 552 77220 8

Originally published in Great Britain by Doubleday,
a division of Transworld Publishers

PRINTING HISTORY
Doubleday edition published 2004
Black Swan edition published 2005

1 3 5 7 9 10 8 6 4 2

Set in 11.5/15.5pt Granjon by
Falcon Oast Graphic Art Ltd.

Black Swan Books are published by Transworld Publishers,
61–63 Uxbridge Road, London W5 5SA,
a division of The Random House Group Ltd,
in Australia by Random House Australia (Pty) Ltd,
20 Alfred Street, Milsons Point, Sydney, NSW 2061, Australia,
in New Zealand by Random House New Zealand Ltd,
18 Poland Road, Glenfield, Auckland 10, New Zealand
and in South Africa by Random House (Pty) Ltd,
Endulini, 5a Jubilee Road, Parktown 2193, South Africa.

Printed and bound in Great Britain by
Cox & Wyman Ltd, Reading, Berkshire.

Papers used by Transworld Publishers are natural, recyclable
products made from wood grown in sustainable forests.
The manufacturing processes conform to the environmental
regulations of the country of origin.

For Virginia

One

It is a full moon and I am sitting on the beach watching a green sea turtle covering her eggs. She rotates slowly, her powerful flippers kicking sand out behind her. It will take two hours for her to turn a full 360 degrees. I am in awe of her, the way she shovels so diligently. She is patient. And she is, with her horny old head, her shell a metre across, beautiful. There are other people here too and as well as being excited I am in a kind of terror that all her work will be for nothing, that the guards standing around with torches will take her eggs not to a hatchery but to a market.

We saw a hatchling from another clutch earlier in the evening, small as a twenty-cent piece, scurrying across the endless desert of sand towards the sea, a pale halo bestowed by the guard's torch as he urged us to 'Look, look quick'. The scene is absurd: four guards, five tourists, twenty locals and this tiny creature running frantically for its life. It is hard, but necessary, to feel hopeful that it will survive.

I turn to the woman next to me, whom I met, as travellers do, at a restaurant earlier this evening.

'Do you think it'll make it?'

She nods, smiling broadly. 'It'll be fine, Catherine.' And there is something about this stranger, this girl, that makes me believe her.

The turtle covers her nest by midnight then heaves herself out of the pit she has dug. She slides down the bank of the nest towards the water but runs out of momentum and must pull herself along the sand for some way. The effort seems enormous and she stops for minutes at a time, too exhausted to move. Finally, she gets close to the water-line and when a wave comes in it picks her up, spins her around and carries her out to sea.

My new friend, Ruby, and I stay on the beach, in our jumpers on a tropical night, talking. We are surrounded by a ghost forest of palm trees, shadows thrown by the coconut grove behind us. The moon is so bright the ocean looks like grey silk, shot with luminous white. It is one of those nights that is so beautiful that you wonder whether you are dreaming it. It is the kind of night people travel weeks and months and years for.

When I ask Ruby her age I find out she is younger than I had thought, only twenty-two to my thirty-seven, but she has something of an old soul about her. She is, in fact, the age I was when I first came to India. Neither of us can really explain why we are sitting in Tangalla, which is basically a tourist resort with attractions as diverse as nesting turtles and child sex. Though there is the fact that the civil war means there are not so many other places in Sri Lanka one can go. This beach in the south of the island is one of the ones that is safe enough. On July 24, just over three weeks ago, the Tamil Tigers attacked the air force base and Colombo's international airport, destroying military aircraft and passenger jets. Twenty-three people were killed.

'So: why Sri Lanka?' Ruby asks. 'Why now?'

I tell her I came to do a meditation retreat, arriving three weeks before the bombing. I hadn't heard about it for a few days, but once the news got around it had seemed to disrupt things and people had started to leave. I ask her why she is here and she tells me she has been working as a volunteer in Colombo for six months, before she goes to India.

So we are both on our way to India and both for the second time. Ruby studied Hinduism at university and wants to spend time in the south, the religion's heartland.

'There is a poem,' says Ruby. 'It's from what you'd call the Hindu version of the Bible. This poem is why I am going back.' She recites, from memory:

> *'You are woman, and you are man,*
> *You are the youth and the maiden,*
> *And the old man tottering with a staff.*
> *You are reborn again facing all directions.*

You are the bluefly and red-eyed parrot,
The cloud pregnant with lightning.
You are the season and the seas,
The Beginning less, the Abiding Lord
From who the spheres are born.'

She pauses, slightly embarrassed.

'I'm glad you're a quoter,' I say. 'Me too.'

'Why are you going back?' she asks and I tell her: because it is a place I dream of even though I have not been there for fifteen years. I tell her that I have travelled to many places. That it was in America that I fell in love, but India that changed everything. What I mean, but can't say to someone I've just met, is that in America I had good sex but in India my spirit was touched. For many years I confused the two and I am finally returning to untangle that knot.

'Tell me,' Ruby says.

'People are bored with stories of obsession. With stories about women in their late thirties who are single, and the reasons why that might be so.' I could have gone on: people are bored with stories about cities and what cities do to people, families and what they do to each other, the perils of geography and the excuses people use to keep others at a distance. When everything was happening, it all made perfect sense to me, but now, despite the clarity of my memories, I don't really understand it at all.

'I like stories,' Ruby says. 'It's one of the fun things about travelling—hearing people's stories.'

'Okay,' I say. 'I will tell you a love story of sorts. I'll tell you a story about the one who drove me crazy. But remember, the main character in this story, she isn't me. Not any more.'

'So who are you now?' she smiles at me.

'I am being reborn again,' I return the smile. 'Facing all directions.'

Just getting on a plane made me want sex. From the moment I sat down and pulled the belt tight there was a heat that grew until all I was aware of was a pulsing, the movement of blood, like my cunt was beating, like it was the very heart of me.

So I was primed by flying before I ever arrived in Los Angeles. Primed by travel, by movement. But even before I left the ground I'd been primed by Michael's suggestive fax: 'Sorry to hear you have a hotel and won't need a bed. Any friend of Marion's…Looking forward to meeting you, call me when you hit town.'

I didn't call him, not straight away. He was a stranger, my housemate's former colleague, and his fax had made me nervous. Its tone seemed to assume something between us, a done deal; or perhaps it was me who assumed, it is hard to tell from this distance. Crazy as it sounds, I knew from the first few words he wrote to me that we would sleep together.

Los Angeles hasn't the graciousness of age, nor the dignity of a long history. But for all the warnings of pollution, I found a city where I could smell desert air and see a broad, blue open sky that reminded me of Sydney, a town I loved; and for all the talk of crassness, in Los Angeles you could feel possibilities, the weightlessness of things that are new. I wanted to live here. On the weekends I'd take my hire car—a 1965 Buick Skylark Convertible that was a dream in itself—and drive around like LA was my very own movie set.

A couple of weeks after I arrived I called my brother, Finn. He was still a long plane ride away; over on the east coast, over in New York where he worked. But at least we were on the same continent now.

'How's LA?' he asked.

'Good. Busy. I've eaten out so much I suspect I am about to turn into a burrito.'

'You have been a burrito for some time.'

'Ignoring that. Did you know I stopped over in Bangkok and saw Dad? We went to see *Groundhog Day*, and then afterwards he said he'd already seen it with you. It's very Buddhist, isn't it? The perfect mix of profound and silly.'

'So we all watched the same film, both of us with Dad. That's very family-like.' I could almost hear him smiling down the phone.

'Everyone told me LA would be awful, but I love it. The architecture is wild and the hotel where I'm staying in West Hollywood is fantastic. All the guys who work here look like Tom Waits and wear shoestring ties. Janis Joplin died here.'

'To be in a hotel that's famous because of a dead person is very cool in the States, you know.'

'I know,' I replied. 'Hey, listen to this.' I'd circled a paragraph in that day's *LA Times*: '*No man should be condemned in this case because of the fear of a riot. My client is on trial. But you are also on trial. Your courage is on trial.*'

'Deep.'

'Fuck off,' I laughed. 'You're a big dork.'

I arranged to meet Michael at a cafe on Melrose. When I walked into the place—all chrome counters and strange macrobiotic salads piled high behind glass—he stood and bowed slightly. I was struck by the particularity of that gesture, the old-fashionedness of it. The other particular thing I noticed was his eyes, an intense blue and all the more compelling for the contrast with his tanned skin. What I said to Marion when I wrote to her next was that his eyes were like Peter O'Toole's in *Lawrence of Arabia*, and she laughed at me of course. But I couldn't stop looking at them, looking into them.

'How does an academic get a tan?' I asked him.

He grinned. 'This is California,' he said. 'Tans are compulsory.'

He was twenty years older than me and he looked it, but the fact that his face was lined, that he was lanky to the point of skinny boniness, and that he retained all the confidence of a good-looking man without the looks themselves, just made me more interested. As lunch went on, I could feel my laugh becoming bigger, my movements more exaggerated, my lips fuller. His life, I thought, is written on his face. And there was something more—this man had slept with a lot of women; I could see that written into his face as well. I remember thinking I wanted to know what that was like, to have had sex with a lot of people. I have read about men like you. I have seen men like you in movies.

We talked. There was an intensity to him, a combination of argumentativeness and attentiveness. He kept touching me on the arm, and once, for a second, on the cheek, with his forefinger as he made his point. I thought he was gorgeous. When I told people about him later I would draw out the vowels of that word: he was *gooorgeous*. I agreed to have dinner with him the next night, kicking myself all the while that I had left it so late in my trip to contact him.

All the next day, I ran this fantasy that he would knock on my hotel room door and that I'd greet him by saying, 'Let's forget dinner. Let's fuck.' All day that was all I thought about. Fucking him.

He was late and I lay on the couch channel surfing until I stumbled over a sitcom about a stand-up comedian.

He was doing a routine on men and commitment. 'When a man is driving down that freeway of love, the woman he's involved with is like an exit, but he doesn't want to get off there…' There was something about ending up on the kerb with smoke pouring out of the engine, but I missed that because Michael walked in. He opened the door without knocking, like he was staying here in the hotel. Like he was staying here with me.

'What's this show?' I turned to him—drew breath, like I always would when I saw him.

'You don't know "Seinfeld"? It's lotsa laughs,' he said. 'Me, I'm a Kramer fan.'

'Kramer? I haven't got to him.' Michael was moving back out the door already, beckoning me with his hand. I followed him out through the lobby.

The streets were full of sirens, everything felt edgy. 'After the police were let off last year, whole suburbs went up in flames,' Michael said. 'According to tonight's news, and I quote, there are 3000 LAPD officers, 1350 Los Angeles County sheriff's deputies, 1500 California Highway Patrol officers, 700 members of the National Guard and assorted others placed at strategic points around the city.' He put an arm around my shoulders and drew me to him briefly. 'We should be safe.'

'We're in the final scene of *The Blues Brothers*, aren't we?' I said. But like everyone I'd seen the video of Rodney King being worked over by police officers and even thousands of miles away in Melbourne I'd found it distressing. I hoped that this time around, the police would be convicted.

After we'd eaten, we cruised down Sunset Boulevard past a bookshop called Book Soup, past bars, past a billboard of Marky Mark muscled, hung and metres tall in his Calvins. Then we drove up through the Hollywood Hills along Mulholland Drive.

'Let me take you somewhere special,' Michael said.

And even though I had driven there myself just a few nights earlier, even though I knew it was a cliché, even though I had seen men drive women to this place so they could make out in more movies than I could count, when Michael stopped at a point where I could see Los Angeles spread out below me, a blanket of lights twinkling like stars, it felt like he had given me a gift. Like it had all been laid out there, especially for me.

I got out of the car and gazed across this cityscape that felt as familiar to me as Melbourne, and more beautiful than I had ever imagined it would be. Michael came up behind me and put a hand on my shoulder. 'There's more,' he said. 'Get back in the car.'

We drove further, then stopped again. I clambered up onto a fence so I was sitting up high and could see the valley spreading out northwards. There was nothing—no hills, curves, coastline—to soften the grid of it, the huge expanse of the San Fernando Valley. It was a city too heavy for the desert it was built on. It was ugly, it was beautiful. I looked into those blue eyes of his and he seemed like this to me as well: ugly and beautiful at the same time.

I was here, with the lights of Los Angeles spread below me. I was here with Michael, holding his hand out to me, to help me step down. I went to take his hand but he leaned forward, held my waist and lifted me into the air. When my feet hit the ground we held onto each other for a moment too long. We looked into each other's eyes. Just like in the movies.

We came down from the hills and drove to some bars in west LA, along Wilshire Boulevard. I was surprised by how closed down the place was—Melbourne would have been livelier at this time of night.

'Everyone's been frightened by the trial,' Michael said, 'but this isn't a great night city at the best of times. People stay home, watch videos—preferably videos starring themselves—then get up early to go to the gym.' He had a dry way of speaking. The way someone speaks if they know a lot and have been a lot of places. He talked to me like I was that kind of person as well, though I was so much younger.

We traded stories about work. He had moved to Los Angeles to study but even though he'd finished his PhD a few years ago he'd stayed on. He'd even scored a green card. I explained my slightly erratic career path from journalist to marketing consultant for a travel agency. 'It merges my favourite things: words and travel,' I told him truthfully, but he looked dubious.

'Academics don't understand marketing,' he said.

'Although the way things are going in universities, we're having to learn.'

Michael told me he had written his PhD on the history of the epistolary form with particular reference to Choderlos Laclos. 'You mean letters?' I asked. 'That's very old-school. I thought it was all about theory these days. Who was Laclos anyway?'

'He wrote *Dangerous Liaisons*. You know the film?'

'Yeah, Malkovich was a total prick. What is it with these films and young girls? Why are men obsessed with virgins?'

'You have to ask?' Michael smiled. 'When they look like Uma Thurman? You're like her, you know. Tall. Blonde, grey eyes, young. What man wouldn't find you attractive?'

'Give it a rest.'

'It's a compliment,' he persisted. 'Women your age think everything is sexist. Everything is about politics, about being politically correct. But that's not what the story is about. It's about desire. It's about love.'

'It's about power, not love.'

'If you can explain the difference to me, I'd be pleased to hear it. People destroy each other. That is what they do. One day you'll understand.' He stopped himself.

I didn't like what he was saying; but he *affected* me. I felt like when I breathed him in, he changed me. He made my heart race, my eyes sting. I wondered if this was what people meant by 'chemistry'.

'You can see why I don't like to talk about my taste in books on the first date,' he said. 'Want another margarita?'

At the end of the night Michael took me along Rodeo Drive. We were driving through Beverly Hills at three or so in the morning when a siren went off behind us and stayed there. Michael pulled over. Drunk, I opened the door to get out of the car and Michael pushed me back into my seat, startling me.

'What are you doing driving around at this hour?' asked one of the cops, the one who was looming—slightly theatrically it seemed to me—over Michael. His gun was in his hand, though, which was not the kind of theatre I wanted to see.

'My friend is new in town, I'm showing her around.'

'Sure.' They stood over him, belligerent, lecturing him to be more careful. Their guns remained in their hands all the while.

After they left Michael sat staring at the wheel. 'I will never, never get used to the police in this country. They really make you feel they could shoot you at any moment. I need a drink.' He turned to me, agitated. 'And what did *you* think you were doing? You could have been shot, trying to get out of the car like that.'

I apologised, put a hand on his arm. 'Come back to my room,' I said. 'I think there's something to drink there.' I was lying, I had no idea if there was anything to drink in my room or not.

As it turned out there wasn't a mini bar. Michael sat

down on the only chair, his head in his hands. 'Let's go to my place. I've got some tequila.'

I sat on the end of the bed, reached out, barely touched the back of his trembling hand with a finger. 'Stay here,' I said.

Michael hesitated a long, long moment before sliding out of the chair and kneeling on the floor before me. He took my face in his hands, and paused again. 'I'm not sure about this,' he said. And then we kissed.

'Feel free to keep trying,' I said, after Michael and I had been having sex for an hour or so, 'but I can tell you now it's not going to happen. Not after hours of drinking. Not the first time.'

'There might not be a second,' he said and I couldn't tell from his voice whether he was joking or not. 'I'd make the most of it if I were you.' It had been a long night. We finally called it quits, the job half done.

'You are beautiful, you know,' he stroked me gently. 'I meant what I said. But you've got more flesh on you than Uma. I like your flesh.'

'One more mention of Uma Thurman and this affair *is* over,' I said, causing Michael to laugh out loud.

'What are you thinking?' he murmured as I was dozing off. As if he had a right to my thoughts and feelings.

'I was thinking about something very corny,' I said. 'About a poem that seems geographically appropriate:

Licence my roving hands, and let them go / Behind, before, above between, below / Oh my America, my new found land.'

I can't believe I said that now, looking back. The things you say when you are young and confident.

'You don't need to quote Donne at me,' Michael rolled me over so my back was to him, spooning in behind me, putting his arm over my waist and placing it between my breasts, pulling me close. 'You've got yourself laid already.'

When I woke he was putting on his socks and shoes. He was polite, but all the intimacy of the night before had evaporated. 'I'll call,' he said, 'about dinner tonight,' but in such a way that I wasn't sure if he would; I couldn't read him at all. My relief when he did call was immense.

We went to a Mexican place that night and I ate chocolate chicken for the first time. Food tasted good around him. Wine went more quickly to my head. All my senses had become more intense in the three days since we'd met.

'I'm going to give you a Hollywood tour,' Michael said, 'then let's go to a movie. I missed *The Piano* the first time around, but since Holly Hunter's won the Oscar I've got a second shot at it.' I didn't tell him I had seen it already. I'd been to Hollywood Boulevard too, though when we got there it was different to the times I'd seen it during the day, looking like a rundown fairground. At night the lights brought it to life, and the shadows covered the seediness.

We started the tour at the corner of Hollywood and

Vine, which, according to Michael, was the centre of Hollywood in the twenties. We zigzagged back and forth across the boulevard and looked at the buildings on either side. We walked past the Frederick's and Newberry Company buildings, in all their art deco glory. Past the Egyptian Theatre, which struck me as having seen much better days. We stopped at the Lee Drug Company building on the corner of Hollywood and Highland to look at the neon Coca-Cola signs set under frosted glass in the pavement of the entrance. We passed the Max Factor Building, the Paramount Theatre and the Masonic Temple.

When we walked past the Chinese Theatre, there was a premiere on with a red carpet and spotlights. I saw Brad Pitt get out of a limousine and I gasped.

'So he does it for you, huh? It's his film that's opening,' Michael said. '*Legends of the Fall*.'

Michael waved at one of the women walking down the carpet, and she smiled back at him.

'Who was that?' I had abandoned attempts to act unimpressed.

'A film producer,' he said. 'Not one you would have heard of.' But she looked like someone I'd have heard of, with her long dark hair and clinging silver gown. I looked down at my own outfit: long grey skirt, flat shoes and a navy polo neck. I began to feel self-conscious.

'That's the forecourt with all the handprints,' Michael said, gesturing off-handedly. 'You have to be a mega star these days to get a shot at it because they're running out of room.'

We went to see *The Piano* at a smaller cinema on Sunset. At the moment Baines fingered the hole in Ada's stocking, there were sharp intakes of breath around the cinema. Michael leant over to me and whispered in the dark, 'Is that power? Or love?'

After the film we went back to Michael's house in Venice. He wandered into the kitchen and I stood in the middle of the living room, awkwardly. Not sure what to do with myself, not sure whether he wanted me to stay or not.

He came back into the room and up to me, standing close, his body almost touching mine. He put two fingers under my chin and lifted it up, forcing me to look into his eyes, then pressed against me gently, pushing me backwards until I felt a table against my thighs. 'Lift your skirt,' he said, placing his hands on my hips and hoisting me up onto the table. I kicked off my shoes and lay back so he could remove my skirt, my underwear. I lay myself out for him. He had a big cock, and though he pushed into me within seconds, I was wet. I had been wet all night.

'Tell me what you want to do,' he whispered into my ear. 'Tell me what you want.' I didn't have courage to say what I was thinking: fuck me hard, fuck me really hard, turn me around, bend me over, fuck me from behind, bite me. But we did all that anyway; he made me feel brave.

We moved from the living room to the bedroom and made love some more, and when we had finished, he whispered, 'Let me stay inside you,' holding me close as he fell asleep.

I lay awake for what was left of the night, hearing the sirens, the helicopters that circled, the ambulances in the distance. I felt safe, surrounded by the sounds of chaos.

I was used to feeling anxious all the time at home, for no reason I could articulate. But here it was different. Anxiety was in the city and its streets, it was in the air—but it was outside, not inside me.

At dawn, I gave up trying to sleep and woke Michael to say good morning, goodbye. We kissed sleepily for a while before I said, 'I've got to go.'

'Don't,' he kissed my neck, reached down and stroked my cunt slowly with the tip of a finger. 'Are you sore?'

'A bit,' I said. I looked at him, at his face even more crumpled than usual by sleep. I gazed at him. He licked the end of his fingers before reaching down again, pushing one gently inside me.

'Too sore to fuck?'

I moaned as he lifted himself onto me. 'Get your aim right,' I whispered, reaching down to hold myself open for him with one hand and position him with the other.

'Now,' I said. 'Push.' And he did, slowly at first because I was raw but then I opened up, and the wet came and he was deep inside me.

'I'll be gentle,' he said.

'Don't be,' I said and after that things became hazy— until, with a jolt, I remembered the time.

'Shit, I'll miss my plane. I've really got to go.' I put my foot against him and lifted him out of me. It was only when I got out of the bed I saw that I had begun to bleed, which was a surprise. Usually when I travelled I stopped menstruating altogether.

'I'll take that as a memento,' Michael said, looking at his ruined sheets. 'Or perhaps some primitive marking of territory. Wait, I'll get up, I'll walk you to the car.'

Disorientated by the sex, by the lack of sleep, I looked the wrong way and stepped out onto the road as a car was bearing down on me. Michael grabbed me by the hand, pulled me back to the footpath.

'What are you doing?' he said. 'Scaring me for the second time.' Then he took my hand and led me over the road like I was a child.

As we walked past the corner store he pointed at a newspaper cage. 'It's over.' The headline on the screamer read, '2 Officers Guilty, 2 Acquitted; Guarded Calm Follows Verdicts in King Case'.

'So,' I said. 'We're safe. I'll see you when I get back to LA?'

'I've got your numbers in New York,' he said. 'I'll call you.'

In the years that followed, I kept thinking back to those first two nights Michael and I spent together, trying to work out the moment that he got under my skin. Trying to pinpoint the moment things shifted from play and romance to obsession. Was it when the sex got good? Was it when he made me feel like an adult? Was it when he made me feel like a child? Was it Los Angeles? I tried to work it out. I wanted to make sure it never happened again.

Two

It looks perfect. Whitewashed, with windows overlooking the ocean. If we looked ceiling-wards we would see there is no fan, but it doesn't occur to us.

'We'll take it,' I say to the owner. She is an elegant, pale Moslem woman dressed from head to foot in white. Her name is Mrs Kalid. She scrutinises us carefully. She is, after all, letting us into her home.

'You may stay,' she nods at us. 'Would you like a Sprite? Or a cup of tea?'

Ruby and I are in Galle. In biblical times King Solomon bought his gems, spices and peacocks here. Now it is a picture-postcard walled town, a tiny place that hasn't changed for centuries. Its fort walls overlook a cricket pitch on one side and the sea on the other.

'This ground is famous,' Ruby says. 'Some very important games have been played here.'

Inside the walls are Dutch churches with blue alcoves,

old colonial hotels with large verandas and whitewashed mosques from which white-robed men pour out at regular intervals. Banyan trees drape over the streets and public squares. It is under one of these trees that we shelter after a storm breaks, though by the time we get there we are soaked already. We huddle together, enjoying the drama of the weather, giggling like young girls. A group of school children are giggling too, as they walk down the street, sharing umbrellas.

'I haven't travelled during the monsoon time before,' I say. 'I had no idea it would be so fun—to start with anyway. I'm sure it would exhaust you after a while. The build-up of humidity all day, the explosion late every after-noon.'

'I've been waiting for this,' says Ruby. 'And now it's come I have to leave it.'

The monsoon is a mystery to me, its beginnings and endings seemingly as variable as the unexpected changes you encounter crossing a street in Manhattan, or climbing down just a few metres into the Grand Canyon. There is no monsoon fifty kilometres east. There is none to the north. But here the clouds tower up above us like skyscrapers, laden with water. Tomorrow we'll leave the rain behind us. Ruby and I have decided to keep travelling across into South India together and, if our travel guides are accurate, will be dancing around three different monsoonal zones.

I don't really know why we have decided to travel

together though I suspect Ruby thinks my age makes me interesting. I like her because she is relaxed, and sure of herself. She doesn't drag history around behind her like I do. We are comfortable with each other.

That night, after we have dried off and dressed up, we head to Sri Lanka's most luxurious hotel, the Lighthouse, for dinner. The columns and patio merge with the rocks and sea below. We order gin and tonics.

'A tuk-tuk driver told me,' Ruby says, 'that not far from here is a famous beach called Sunset Point.' She leans forward and points to our left, to a cove some kilometres away. 'And, this man says, on that beach Arthur C. Clarke, David Hasselhoff and Lord Mountbatten have all stood. He said these men's names in one breath, as if they were all equally significant. David Hasselhoff—who remembers him?'

I laugh. 'I remember him,' I say. 'I was a big "Night Rider" fan and I even saw his fine performance this year in *Shaka Zulu: The Citadel*.'

'Well,' Ruby says drily. 'Let's change the subject so I can continue to respect you.'

Ruby tells me she is intimidated by how much I have travelled and I tell her that I travelled a long way and to many places without getting anywhere. That I worked overtime to impose an order on things no matter how far I strayed from home.

Ruby isn't buying it, doesn't believe I'd still be travelling if it were just a form of narcissism. She says there is nothing wrong with being younger and making young-people mistakes.

'We all stuff up,' she says.

I hesitate. I'm not sure I know her well enough to ask her what her mistakes might be. Me, I'm talking about my past because I am shedding it. She is watching me slough off my old skin.

We order more drinks. The humidity makes us drink quickly and the gin and tonic is working its effect. Ruby asks me how I imposed order on things.

'Perhaps it's a journalist thing,' I say. 'I have a series of grids. When I travel I read the papers, watch TV and get caught up in any local media event. Afterwards I organise the event—in my head anyway—according to the decade it happened in, and the place, and, more bizarrely, the man I was seeing at the time. It is like playing with building blocks. Building things, creating meaning, to soothe oneself.'

Ruby raises an eyebrow. 'Have you heard of Obsessive Compulsive Disorder?'

'Like this,' I recite my litany in a sing-song voice. 'I was born in the sixties, and that is when I first went to America and that is when my parents separated. I was at high school in the seventies, I got a new dad, and there was Cyclone Tracy. I studied journalism in the eighties. I fell in love with my geography teacher, our family ended all over again, there was the Ash Wednesday bushfires and I went to India. I worked for a travel agency in the nineties and I met Michael. And Max was born. There were bushfires and earthquakes and blizzards. I came to Sri Lanka in the new century—a girl like me loves it when there is an actual new century—and the airport was blown up.

'You see how neat everything is?'

'A new dad?' asks Ruby. 'How many do you have?'

'Two. I call my first father Father, and my second father Dad.'

'So it's like this,' Ruby says. 'We are sitting in a hotel in Sri Lanka in August, 2001, and it's your turn to buy the drinks.'

We go back to our room to find that it has heated up like an oven. 'No fan,' Ruby grimaces. 'And these windows, they don't open. There is only this grille at the top.'

We lie on our beds, tossing and turning; it's partly the drink but mainly the heat. Our beds are only six inches apart and I can hear Ruby's every move, her efforts to rearrange her limbs as she seeks out the cooler parts of the sheet. Her low moans of frustration and irritation. I periodically fall into a half sleep and sweaty dreams full of dread. Telling Ruby my story is making my time with Michael come back to me with the kind of intensity I haven't felt for years. I am restless with rushes of loathing, not desire. I cannot believe I let this happen, that I lost those years. I won't tell Ruby everything, I can't, but even in the partial telling I find I remember more.

At around three a.m. I say, 'Do you ever feel that you've

been beaten by something that other people think is quite trivial? And then you hate yourself twice over: for being defeated, and for the cause being so…nothing…compared to what most people deal with in their lives?'

'It's not a competition,' she says; then, after we have lain silent for a few moments, 'Let's go outside and walk around the fort walls. It will be beautiful at this time of night.' I pull on my clothes. She takes me down the street to the 340-year-old battlement walls that look across palm trees and rocks and ocean, all grey silver white in the moonlight. She takes me outside, where it's cool.

The first time I was in Los Angeles my mother and father tried to make me walk out of the airport into the carpark, but the noise—people, planes, taxis and buses—upset me and I had to be carried, like a baby. It is hard for me to remember details. I can remember that I stared through the taxi windows, at the Los Angeles suburbs sprawling out and away.

I know, because I was told, that we caught the train from San Francisco to Boston. I don't know how we got to San Francisco, though when I drove down Highway 101 almost thirty years later, along the coast and through Big Sur, I thought I could remember the landscape from this time, from when I was little. But memory does that. Makes you think things have happened that maybe never did.

The train we caught was red and we were on it for three days and two nights. We slept on little foldout beds attached to the wall and it felt like magic to me, like living in a doll's house. I remember that I spent most of the time reading books of my favourite fairy tales: *Sleeping Beauty*, *Cinderella*, *Snow White*.

We changed trains in Chicago, the day of the Chicago riots in 1968, the ones where the yippies got squirted with firemen's hoses and put flowers into the ends of the soldiers' guns. This is something I've been told, by history books and my father. My father likes to remember things as events, as newsworthy and I'm left with his exaggerated sense of things in lieu of memory, or facts.

When I watch the footage of this on the television, years later, it seems strange to me that I was in that place on that day, moving through history without it touching me. My father and everyone else his age seemed trapped in those times, defined by them; this falling away of all that they knew. To me change was a constant, so that when I grew up it seemed to me that I did not know how to stand still.

We'd gone to America so my father could study journalism at Columbia University. One day soon after we arrived he took me there. People were wearing beads and badges and the men had long hair. That day at the university people were upset because Robert Kennedy had just been assassinated.

'He's the brother of the man who was assassinated the day you were born,' my father told me.

'What's assassinated?' I asked.

'It means that someone has killed you and you are dead,' my father said.

'What's dead?'

I can't remember now what answer he gave, but the memory of asking the question came to me vividly when I was in India that first time. Death was everywhere and I spent two weeks with amoebic dysentery. I was twenty-two, but felt like a child. Frightened, and wishing someone else would come and help me sort out this mess, the mess of everything going wrong a long way from home. I realise now that that is how my parents felt when they were in America. That they were too young to deal with this, that everything was going wrong, that they were a long way from home.

When I was four, I sat at a breakfast bar in New York and was asked what kind of cereal I wanted. I remember looking up at the shelf behind the waitress and seeing little cardboard packets of all different kinds of cereal. 'What are they?' I pointed.

'Variety Packs.'

Choice: I could have cocoa pops or rice bubbles or cornflakes. I was four years old sitting on a barstool in Manhattan and could choose whatever breakfast cereal I wanted. Freedom in breakfast cereal didn't happen in

Melbourne in the 1960s. After the Variety Packs my mother and father took me to Central Park and bought me a Mickey Mouse balloon full of helium. When I let it go it floated in the air, up and up, until it was gone. You didn't get those in Melbourne either.

My mother bought me a little wicker table and chair that sat by my new bed. My dolls slept on the table. I can still remember waking up one morning, when things smelt new, to find that my new dolls and furniture had disappeared and my mother was packing our bags. So, for a few years anyway, that was another thing New York had that Melbourne didn't. My father.

That was an early lesson. Men I loved disappeared for no reason. They lived in other places, a long way away. There was another lesson in that as well. Don't ask men why they do these things. These things just happen, and, they tell you, everyone tells you, it doesn't mean they don't love you. Things just happen.

When I arrived in Los Angeles the second time, the time I met Michael, I hired a car and headed for West Hollywood. I had been on a plane for fifteen hours, was jetlagged and disorientated. I had never driven on the wrong side of the road before. I ended up, two hours later, in Inglewood, where riots had taken place a year before. I drove another seven miles to Santa Monica, though that hadn't been where I was heading either, and ordered coffee and a ranch salad. It seemed that since the Variety Pack days the notion of choice had got a little out of control. I was asked whether I wanted blue cheese dressing, French, Italian or ranch. For my coffee I was offered white liquid that was low in fat or high, as well as sugar or low-calorie sweeteners. 'Normal fat,' I wanted to say. 'Just normal.' I was tired. I didn't know what I wanted.

I collect maps, have I told you that? I have maps for driving tours of Ireland and walking tours of Spain. Other maps show me where there might be a swell of land, a hill, a mountain. Relief maps, they were called in Geography. I have maps that show you where to find family clans in Scotland and the areas particular Aboriginal languages are spoken. I have maps that show me the last bits of the world where you might find a tiger in the wild, that show me where different species of birds migrate to and from and where whales swim as they move up the east coast of Australia.

I didn't have a decent map of Los Angeles, though. The streets, hills and canyons of Los Angeles were familiar to me, had formed the streetscapes of most of the films I had seen. I felt as if I would know my way around. But Los Angeles, as it turns out, was the place where I needed a map most of all. It was a place I got lost.

There is a moment, driving in from JFK airport, when you cross the Triborough Bridge and suddenly see Manhattan spread out before you, just like in the opening credits of a film. When I arrived in Manhattan the second time, just after my affair with Michael had begun, I felt a sudden rush of feeling when we got to that bridge, like I was crossing over into the centre of all that was important.

The bus dropped me at Grand Central and I caught the train down to SoHo, where Finn lived. He took me to eat Indian on Sixth Street, but I was so tired I almost fell asleep in the lamb korma.

'I'll become interesting and worthy of siblinghood tomorrow,' I said. 'I promise.'

'Actually, I'm used to you being boring,' said Finn. 'But is there a particular reason behind how thoroughly boring you're being tonight? Is it your lack of excitement at not having seen me for over a year?'

'There are two reasons: reason one is that I am so comfortable around you that you bring out my inner bore. Reason two is that I spent all last night having sex with a guy called Michael and…'

Finn flung his hand into the air, like a traffic policeman. 'I'm your brother. No details please. But is this a "I'm in LA so I'm going to have an international quickie" thing, or will you see him again?'

'We might meet up in Phoenix and go to the Grand Canyon together.'

'Is he based permanently in LA?' Finn asked.

'I think,' I said. 'He teaches at UCLA.'

'Sounds good,' he said. 'You could be like those Chinese guys I just read about in *Maximum City*.'

'Excuse me?' I asked. Knowing the way Finn's mind

worked, I hoped this was going to be good. '*Maximum City?*'

'A history of New York. The author talks about Chinese men who came to New York around the turn of the century to earn a living, but they weren't allowed to bring any family out. So they'd marry a woman in China, stay three months, hopefully impregnate her in that time, then head to New York. They'd return to China three years later to meet their children, and, after that, maybe never see them again. The wives were called living widows.

'So some guy lives in Manhattan, running a laundry, living alone in a single room, and in Manhattan he's no one. But he knows he's someone back home in China where he has a family and maybe owns some land, so he doesn't care so much what the New Yorkers think.'

'Are you saying if I kept up with Michael I could have my very own chance to be a living widow?'

'No, you strike me as the man,' said Finn. 'Working in the laundry, hanging out in gambling halls. A secretly rich and powerful guy who has a whole world—well, a whole family—in his head.'

'Ahh, thank you, Grasshopper,' I bowed low. 'You are a very wise man and I must remember to discuss my love life with you more often. Perhaps you'll now allow me to go home and meditate in silence on what you say?'

Once we were back at Finn's apartment I ran a bath, put foam into the steaming water and stepped into it. I started reading a current edition of *Vanity Fair* but had also moved the television into the bathroom so I could watch 'Melrose Place'. I learnt that Alison was going to win Billy over Amanda, and that Michael and Kimberly were having an affair that was being conducted, for the most part, in an elevator. Knowing these things a full six months before those episodes were in Australia felt like the height of sophistication. This is what I thought as I lay in the bath: *My name is Catherine Monaghan. I am in a bathtub, in New York, New York, The United States of America, The World, The Universe.*

The next morning Finn took me to Dean and Deluca's for breakfast, and I made another discovery. Strawberry muffins.

Finn looked more noticeably Australian than he did back home. He was tall, like me. Determinedly anti-fashion, he was wearing a flannelette shirt, Blundstone boots and the beginning of a beard. 'This place is a bit of a wank,' he said. 'But I thought you'd like it.'

'Yes, well struggle through that excellent short black for my sake.' I stuck out my tongue, then decided that since I was twenty-seven and in a restaurant in New York I should try and act more grown up.

Once Finn had left for work I made a plan to take myself from one end of the island to the other. I caught the train down to the World Trade Center and climbed it. I floated in the sky of the city and gazed at it spread below. Then I walked down to Battery Park and looked at the

Statue of Liberty. From there I walked, slowly, to Union Square, where I had a coffee.

Walk one block in Manhattan, even half a block, and everything changes and I liked that, that you couldn't predict what was around the corner. My nerves were on edge, alive. Michael had done that to me, New York was doing it to me. I felt as if I had pins and needles all over my body no matter what I was doing: walking, looking in shops, looking at art. Every brush against my skin, the movement of fabric over my flesh, made me flinch.

At Union Square I moved down to the subway and as the train sped through its tunnels I wondered what part of the city was above me—was I passing under the Chrysler Building? Would the weight of it crush me? I stared out the train windows into the darkness and imagined I could see the homeless, the mad, the devastated who lived underground in the network of tunnels and crannies that had been left when the subway was dug at the end of the last century.

I emerged on West 125th, and walked past the Apollo Theatre, the hair braiding shops and the street markets until I found Sylvia's where I ate southern fried chicken, greens and mash. Everyone had told me not to walk through Harlem, that it would be dangerous, but no one hassled me. I walked until I found the Addicts Rehabilitation Choir a few blocks away. The choir was singing gospel and within minutes I was on my feet, clapping and dancing.

'God lives here, yes he does,' the preacher shimmied through the crowd. 'He moves through us all.'

'Yes,' I sang with everyone. 'Yes he surely does.'

'Where you from?' the preacher came up to me, 'where do you call home?'

'The world,' I sang into the mike, full of joy all of a sudden. 'The world is my home.'

I had planned to go out dancing on my first night in Manhattan, but I'd exhausted myself. Finn took me to the Odeon for an early dinner.

'More expensive groove for you,' he said.

'I don't need groove,' I retorted. 'I almost found God today. In Harlem.'

Finn burst out laughing. 'I have consulted with the lord,' he said shortly, when he had recovered himself. 'And the lord says stick to sex.'

'Fuck you,' I smiled beatifically.

After dinner Finn and I sat, gripped, watching the drama unfold at Waco. We watched the troops built up around the fort in Texas. Listened to the commentators who described a people becoming more and more entrenched in their position, a cult that would rather die than surrender, victims of a megalomaniac who had no care for their lives.

'How could they do it,' I asked. 'Hand over all responsibility to Koresh?'

'They all think they'll be resurrected, so death doesn't scare them,' said Finn. 'I didn't understand how many crazy cults there were in this country till I got here. Everyone's desperate to give their lives over to someone.'

Before I went to bed that night I wrote a long letter home to Marion.

'Confession time,' I wrote. 'I told you that I thought Michael had eyes like Peter O'Toole, but what I didn't tell you is that we did more than flirt. I'm going to use big words here: I think he is *the one*. Does that sound ridiculous? But something has shifted in me—it's as though there's been some kind of chemical reaction and all the fluids in my body are somehow re-tuned to flow towards him. And now I'm in New York, in such a daze that I feel like I've had a lobotomy. Simone de Beauvoir wrote about this in *The Second Sex*—after she started sleeping with Sartre she became so obsessed that even getting on the tram became an erotic experience for her. I know how she felt, like everything around you is penetrating you— forgive the pun—the music, the art, the funk of the subway. Everything turns into sex.'

Marion teased me about the letter for a long time after that. 'You didn't waste any time slotting yourself and Michael into some great romantic tradition. Chemical reaction? Re-tuned body fluids? De Beauvoir and Sartre? He's old and a bit smart, and you're young and smart. There the resemblance ends.'

*

I spent the next day at MOMA. I got home that afternoon and put on the TV just as the tanks moved towards the compound and it erupted in flames. You could hear the screams, see people on fire as they leapt out of windows trying to escape the flames. There was the odd gunshot as some contrived to cut short their suffering. Eighty-six people died. It was not clear to me why the government thought killing these people was a way of saving them. In their own way they were as crazy as Koresh.

Finn got home as I was watching a blow-by-blow news report of what had happened. 'That Michael guy sent a fax for you to my work number,' he handed me the fax, before turning to the TV. 'He likes to keep things enigmatic, doesn't he?'

'I don't mind enigmatic.'

'I can't believe the government went in like that,' Finn wasn't listening. 'It's insane.'

But I was no longer watching the TV.

'Catch a plane to Phoenix,' said the fax. 'I have five days. I'll meet you at the Desert Sands Hotel, May 4, 4 p.m. We can tour around from there. M.'

Three

'Fact: this is where the Australian cricketers drink,' Ruby tells me, as we sit in the bar of the Galle Face Green Hotel, drinking a midday beer. The tropics do that to you.

'Counter fact: Bombay has the largest film industry in the world. Bigger than Hollywood.'

'It's Mumbai, not Bombay. Bombay is part of India's colonial past. Mumbai is the future. You can be a know-it-all, but sometimes I know more.' Ruby thrusts her fist into the air as if she has just taken a wicket. '*Yes.*'

'I know you think it's funny, but it does seem like only yesterday that I was there, and it was called Bombay. And you're not helping,' I say, half accusing, half teasing. 'On the second day we met you asked me if I was alive when Gough Whitlam was sacked.'

Ruby laughs out loud and I realise I like watching her, even when she is provoking me: the way she throws her head back to laugh, her pale freckled face, her broad mouth.

'I just want to know,' Ruby continues to stir me, 'whether historical moments you've lived through have felt big when they happened. Like being alive when Marilyn Monroe died. Or Kennedy was assassinated. Or even seeing Kashmir before it was destroyed?'

I say that the shimmering light and water of Kashmir seemed timeless and that it never occurred to me that things could change. Kashmir felt outside of history, floated out of time, like things do when you are in love. It is only when the affair is over that you realise months or years have gone by, and, sometimes, what was beautiful has been laid waste. I tell her that she should know how these things feel, what with her months in Colombo. She refused to go home when the government urged all Australians to leave the country; now she has developed a habit of starting whenever she hears a loud noise. She's cut short her time here for that reason.

'I wasn't born when Marilyn died,' I say. 'But I was born the very day Kennedy was killed. November 22, 1963. My mum tells me that she couldn't sleep because the radios in the hospital were never turned off.'

'Did you have to spend every birthday watching footage of Jackie picking the top of JFK's head off the back seat of the limo?' Ruby asks.

She is right, I did. And I wonder whether that is why media events are one of my organising principles. I wonder if that is why I became a journalist. There are the big moments; those things that happen that make everyone draw breath, make them realise that at any moment anything and everything could change—cyclones, wars, a man walking on the moon, bushfires, sudden deaths and earthquakes. The things that happen in the world that mean for a few moments a lot of people are talking about the same thing and for a few moments there is the illusion of community. Then there are the smaller events that act like punctuation points: songs, films and television shows.

We discuss whether this really is community. I used to think it was but now am not so certain. Ruby thinks it is, a sharing of experience as people talk about what they have seen and heard. I wonder whether it is just a kind of perving.

'When did you ever actually do something as a result of seeing something on TV?' I ask her, and she stumps me by saying, 'Now. That's why I'm in Sri Lanka. I saw a documentary about the civil war and decided to go and help out for a while.' As she talks I realise I'm touchy on this subject because the more I've watched, the less I've done.

'You sound like one of those old "TV is evil" fogies,' says Ruby.

'I'm becoming one,' I admit. 'I recently worked out how many hours I'd spent in front of the box. Assuming two hours a day every day from the age of five—which is probably an underestimate—the answer is 23,496 hours.

That's almost three years of my life in front of the television. Four if you allow for sleeping at night.'

'Time for more screen action, then,' Ruby says, downing her beer. 'You must be feeling deprived.'

We're heading off to watch four hours of pulsating melodrama, singing, dancing and cricket: *Lagaan*. We walk down the road to the Liberty Cinema and it's a shock to be out of the airconditioning. Colombo is hot, hotter than anywhere else we've been in Sri Lanka. Rolls of barbed wire signal military checkpoints every fifty metres or so. The roads are pocked with large potholes and some are shut off altogether. Everything looks battered, ruined, closed down.

'Should I be excited about a film whose title translates as "Land Tax"?' I ask.

'You should be very excited.' Indeed Ruby can hardly contain her excitement and is speaking with great animation. 'Indian film reviewers have described it as the best film *ever* made in the entire *history of the world*. The climax is one hour and twelve minutes of cricket.'

'That pleases you?' I ask.

'Very much.' She puts on a Sri Lankan accent. 'Shane Warne,' she nods her head thoughtfully. 'Ricky Ponting,' she beams. 'Adam Gilchrist. Muttiah Muralitharan. Sanath Jayasuriya,' she raises her eyebrows theatrically. 'In those names, with appropriate hand and facial gestures, a whole world of conversation lies.'

*

It is an expansive and joyful film, it makes us happy. Ruby dances out of the cinema, doing a kind of sideways Indian rumba down the street and moving her head from side to side. We sing the words from one of the film's songs as we move our way back towards Galle Road:

> *Black clouds, black clouds, shower down rain!*
> *Let loose not the sword of lightning, but the arrows of rain-drops!*
> *Our difficult days have passed; brother, play for us the songs of the monsoon!*
> *Our minds and bodies will be soaked by the rain of love.*

As Ruby sings 'soaked by the rain of love' she runs her hands over her body in a sexy, comic way, putting all her emphasis into the final word of the sentence. She sings 'lerv' instead of 'love'. People stop and stare.

We get to Galle Face Green and stop for a moment. Our exuberance has slowed and we are hot again. We stand and look up at the sky, as the characters in *Lagaan* do after their dance is finished and the clouds have moved on without unloading themselves. Parched in the heat, waiting for rain.

I would tell friends the story of the start of my affair with Michael like a recitation of great moments in pop culture.

The fact that I watched my first ever 'Seinfeld' episode the night we got together. The fact he had eyes like Peter O'Toole. The fact that Janis Joplin died in the hotel I was staying in. The fact that it was the night before the Rodney King verdict came down. As if these dramas were connected to us, to our passion.

The rugged American landscape conspired to make our time together seem even more iconic. We met at the Grand Canyon and drove around Monument Valley, the location for John Ford's *The Searchers*. We made love in a desert town where a killer was born, and that night there was a full moon.

When I retell the story I slip between what happened to me and what was happening around me. Solid facts anchored the affair, earthed the tentative messages that were sent over the years: down phone lines, by fax, by email, the occasional old-fashioned postcard. Gave weight to those seconds when his hand sat in the small of my back, when the lightness with which he held me suggested the most delicate, the most fragile of feelings. I built a relation-ship, block by block, from words and weather, the phases of the moon, pieces of movies, and media soundbites.

It was four in the afternoon and I'd been sitting around in my motel room in Phoenix for hours waiting for Michael to arrive. He was late, though he'd warned me he might be. He had a long way to drive. I was becoming nervous. Could you really make an arrangement to meet someone you hardly knew in the middle of Phoenix and have them turn up?

There was a knock on the door. I opened it and Michael was standing there, grinning at me, a bottle of cold beer in his hand. I had it again, that feeling of my breath catching when I looked at him. Actually, the word to use would be swooned. I swooned to see him. He kissed me on the cheek as he walked in, pulled off his baseball cap and ran his fingers through his hair. He looked tired. 'I haven't had a shower and I've been driving for ten hours. Am I too dirty to kiss?'

I put my swooning to good use and fell upon the bed. 'Dirty enough to fuck, I'd say.'

'That's the kind of welcome I was hoping for,' he said, laughing for a moment before becoming intent. He rested one hand on my hip and undid his fly with the other.

'Wait,' I said, and got off the bed while he stood there, hard. I pulled off my shoes, my jeans, before getting back onto the bed, turning my arse towards him. 'Now.'

'Jesus,' he groaned, as he slid into me. 'I'm going to have to try not to come straight away.' I ground against him, lowered my body so I was at such an angle that he could get in deeper.

'That is not helping…Not helping at all.'

I felt sluttish and horny and other things, things I couldn't put words to. I felt like some kind of animal. I wanted to taunt him. After a few minutes I lifted my fore-arms so I was on all fours, and thrust my body hard up against his pelvis with each word I spoke. 'If. You. Keep. Fucking. Me. So. Hard,' I said, 'Of. Course. You. Are. Going. To. Come.'

I could feel Michael breathing heavily, unsure whether he should slow down or go faster. I slammed against him. He gasped, pulled out and onto my back, curving his body over mine, pulling me tight against him. I could feel him pulsing against me, the heat of his cum spreading out over my back.

'You're not big on foreplay, are you?' I said, when he had recovered.

'And you're not big on drawing things out,' he smiled. 'Foreplay is fine, if you haven't been thinking about someone several times a day for three weeks.' He stroked my hair. 'For a girl who didn't say much last time we fucked, you weren't stuck for words.'

'I've had three weeks to think about things as well.'

'No one should come to America,' Michael said, 'and not see the Grand Canyon.' And he was right. Nothing could have prepared me for its scale and grandeur. Words fell away in the face of it and I stood in silence, we both did, watching the setting sun darkening the walls, throwing shadows, turning stone dark red, purple and then, suddenly, briefly, gold.

That night I sat in bed and read my guidebook. There were so many facts about the place, so many stories; I wanted to know them all. '*The Grand Canyon is 277 miles* long, a mile deep and as much as eighteen miles wide,' I quoted at Michael from *The Time-Life Book on the Grand Canyon*.

'*All of it has been carved out by erosion—by the River Colorado and the subtle but overpowering forces of snowflakes, raindrops and air.*'

Michael was watching basketball on the television with the sound down. He turned around attentively—enough to make me pursue my search for facts that read like poetry. '*At its deepest point, along the stretch known as Granite Gorge, the Canyon slices about a mile into the earth's crust and 2000 million years into its past.* That is very, very, cool. *Before the Colorado was dammed, it surged along at speeds and in volumes great enough to carry an average of 500,000 tons of rocky debris and sediment each day. In flood conditions the current could actually carry six-foot boulders.*'

Michael, looking at me, was all smile lines and eyes. He reached out to me and I put my book down.

The next morning we went to Mather Point to watch the sun come up behind Vishnu Temple. There are many outcrops called temples in the canyon: Brahma, Siva, Buddha and Manu. The outcrops were first isolated by erosion and then attacked by weathering on all sides. Early explorers felt that the peaks looked like oriental temples, so that is how they named them.

Despite my pleasure in that place, I struggle now to remember the beauty of it. It is the sex Michael and I had as we travelled that is bright in my memory, everything else is dim. What I remember as if it happened yesterday is stopping on old Route 66, pushing my seat back as far as I could with Michael crouched down between my thighs while my feet were on his shoulders. His fingers were inside me. His tongue as well. Disconcertingly I caught a glimpse of my face, contorted with pleasure, in the rear vision mirror, then, more disconcertingly still, I noticed a truck had pulled off the road a few metres ahead and the driver was watching us. I touched Michael's hair. 'You'd better stop,' I murmured, 'We've been spotted.' Michael lifted his head for only a moment, his face dripping with me, before going down on me again.

We drove through the day, hands touching knees. We would sit in silence then chat in bursts.

'Here's a game Marion used to play, she probably played it with you: if there was a movie about your life,' Michael asked, 'who would you want to play you?'

I got a shock when he asked that because that is exactly what I had been thinking. That I was in a road movie with my dangerous and sexy lover. 'When I played that game with Marion last I said Jane Fonda, *Klute* era. Now I'm thinking Julie Christie.'

'Not bad,' he said. 'Could be. But she's too old now. You need to think of someone younger. Uma Thurman?'

'Fuck off,' I laughed. 'And you?'

'John Malkovich, of course.'

*

PM Dawn was on the tape deck, floaty, insistent. *Reality used to be a friend of mine.* Through the windows I could see cacti, they were blooming and I had never realised before that their flowers were so perfect and delicate. Over the hours the landscape shifted, the earth heaved up, there were rocks scattered about in clumps, more and more gashes in the earth. Everything had been flat to the horizon but now there were mountains.

No one had told me about the painted desert so it was the most lovely surprise to see the mounds of earth striped through with pastel colours: pink, beige, yellow, pale grey, blue. We drove through Navajo territory and stopped at Betatakan, the Navajo National Monument. We looked at the honeycomb dwellings of the Anasazi, carved deep into the canyon wall.

'They only lived here for a century or so, around the thirteenth century. No one really knows what happened. They think they ran out of water. And who can live without water?' Michael was standing formally, reading to me from a brochure he had picked up from the visitors' centre. With his reading glasses pushed down his nose and the seriousness of his delivery, I could imagine what he would be like standing in a lecture theatre. Smart and sexy and a little bit vulnerable. I walked up to him and put my arms around him, kissed the side of his neck.

'I don't know that I've ever been to such a special place.'

'You can see why the new-agers love it so much

around here,' he said. 'There is a lot of talk of "energy lines".' He spoke in a deliberately dry, ironic tone. To make sure, I suppose, that I didn't think he believed any of this stuff, even though I had caught him reading his star signs in the paper only the day before.

'Why are you single?' I asked him on one long stretch of road.

'The inevitable question,' he said shortly. 'You lasted longer than most. I was married to an American woman. I met her when I first got the position over here. She was in one of my tutorial groups. A student. Your age probably. The full cliché.'

'What was her name?'

'Roberta. We were together for five years. That was partly how I got my green card and why I stayed after my scholarship ran out, but that's not why we married. We were in love. Well, I was. She met someone else, over a year ago now. And—this is where the joke is on me—he was an Australian, and she lives there now. Somewhere in Queensland. As far as she was concerned I went from being this really interesting sexy older guy who knew a lot about books, to an ageing roué who spent all his time in stuffy libraries.' He stopped abruptly. 'Can we not talk about this?'

I didn't listen, I pushed too hard. I asked him whether he'd ever considered coming home when he separated from his wife.

'Home?' he asked, sarcastic now. 'Where's that?' There was a long pause and then, 'I mean it. Where is home to you?'

I found I didn't know what to say. Melbourne was the place from which I went out and away—to America, to India, to men and places I didn't know. 'A friend…all right, to be honest, a lover, my geography teacher, made me think of it this way. Melbourne is the place where I can trace the lines of affection.'

'Exactly,' says Michael. 'And they are the lines that we can get tangled in. They are what must be avoided.' Michael understood ambivalence. That made me believe he understood me. 'America,' Michael said, 'is easier.'

'It wasn't easier the first time I came here,' I said. 'Like you, I was left here. But for some reason I don't blame the place. Not like I blame Melbourne. I suppose that doesn't make sense.'

'It's always easiest to blame the places and people who are closest to you.'

These are some of the things that happened to me and Finn the first time we were in New York: when we got there we lived in an apartment, not a quarter-acre block with a Hills Hoist. There was no garden and we didn't have a cat. We didn't go out and play on the street either because my mother said it was dangerous and we didn't live there long because soon it was the day when I got up to see where my table and doll had gone.

I found my mother in the bathroom brushing her teeth. I stood watching her while she spat the toothpaste out into the basin. She got some in her hair. I don't know where Finn was, though he was only two, he must have been close by.

'Where is my doll?' I asked my mother. 'Why are there so many boxes?'

'We're going home.'

'Why are we going home?' I asked but my mother did not answer, just held on to the basin. 'Where's home?' I asked. 'Isn't home here?'

'It's Melbourne,' she said.

I went to find my father, to ask him why we were going home. He was in the television room, surrounded by more boxes. I asked, 'Why are you crying? Is it because we are going home?' and he said, 'Yes.' Then he said that he was not going with us. That he was sad.

I tried to nail things down: 'Will you be coming in one day? Will you be coming in two weeks?' and my father said, no, maybe he wouldn't come for years. I didn't understand what that meant, because years...well, years was as old as me.

He hugged me and rocked me, both of us crying. I ran to my mother, told her, 'Mummy, Daddy is crying,' and my mother just stood there, leaning against the basin, her long blonde hair hanging, toothpaste smeared over her mouth. I can remember this, her sad and lovely face, as if it was yesterday. My mother was much younger than I am now.

I cannot imagine having two children at twenty-five. I am thirty-seven and still feel like a child myself.

That day tangled things up for me—things like love and absence; who leaves and who stays behind and what it means—and they got more tangled ten years later when my second dad left. People don't like it when you talk about this, not when almost everyone has been divorced or is going to be and is freaking out about what it is they are doing to the kids. This is what you are never meant to ask: why didn't you stay together because of me, *for* me? Why can't you stay together forever? Why am I not the centre of your world?

We drove through Monument Valley at dawn. When we got there in the pale light of the morning, the sun not yet above the horizon, it was not only as I had seen in films, it was as I had seen it in my own ad, the one I'd designed for work: monolithic rocks soaring out of a desert floor that was flat and hard and dry. I imagined what it must have been like millions of years before when the desert was the bottom of the ocean, and the sandstone had not yet eroded. I closed my eyes and I was flying around the jutting rocks, an eagle—no, a condor. I closed my eyes again and I was swimming through an underwater valley. It was then that the sun rose and suddenly everything was gold, dazzling me.

'You can practically see John Wayne, can't you,' Michael said, 'riding out to save his niece before she's despoiled by the Comanche.' He grabbed me and kissed me with stagey brutality. 'Makes me feel like a real man. Makes me feel like despoiling something.'

I pushed him away. This was one moment when the landscape enraptured me more than Michael.

It was two days' hard driving back to Los Angeles and we stopped in a strange little town in the middle of the desert to sleep. Kingman—the birthplace of Timothy McVeigh, although nobody would hear of him for another two years.

That night we both went straight to sleep, exhausted. I woke some hours later to feel Michael hard against me, half-moving, half-asleep. There were such gentle strokes and touches and movements between us I couldn't tell where he ended and I began. By the time we were properly awake, I was on top of him and he was inside me. He lightly scratched the small of my back and I arched, as if I were a cat.

'I could fuck you forever,' I said. 'I *want* to fuck you forever,' then regretted my intensity.

'I don't know why,' Michael undercut his abruptness by reaching up and kissing me on the lips. It was dark, I couldn't see his expression and perhaps because I wanted it so much it seemed to me that perhaps he felt the same way. That he wanted things to last forever as well.

We made love again back in Venice the next afternoon, the day I was to leave, with a kind of feather-light touch that felt like love. He looked at me, for a long time, and I managed to look back without flinching. Before this afternoon I had always had to turn away from the intensity of his gaze.

He rested his face against me, breathed on me. Touched me gently with his tongue. 'Please,' I said.

Then: 'Now.'

We moved together for a while before he said, 'I can't. I'm too sad that you are leaving.' So we kissed and talked. For a while we slept. When I moved away from him, he pulled me back towards him, put his hand on my cheek. 'I could love you,' he said. 'Perhaps I already do.' And the words filled me up.

We drove to the airport, stopping in a bar on the way for a beer and something to eat. 'Try this beer,' he said. 'It's called Bohemia, it's Mexican.' And I did, loving the colour and taste of it. I can still remember how it tasted all these years later.

At the airport Michael had tears in his eyes. 'Being with you reminds me of home.'

I never really got to know Michael. But I came to know distance intimately and to understand what it did to desire; I came to understand that desire was as much a place as any country I had visited. It had its own geography. At first I thought it was just me but over the years I learnt that Michael was lost in this place as well. With him I visited the dreamscapes that had nourished me since I was a child. Distance, desire, ambivalence, city, they were all one. And always there was the fact that he was eight thousand miles away, the fact that it was impossible, the fact that distance stretched our desire so taut I thought I might die of longing.

Four

When I wake on the morning we are to leave for India, Ruby is lying in the next bed, bald. Her hair, when she had it, was long, curly and red. It reached halfway down her back.

She laughs when she sees my face. 'I suddenly realised,' she says, 'that my hair was a vanity. I shaved it all off.'

'Are you sure that's not just the hash talking?'

'No, I'm not,' she says. 'But it's too late to worry about that now.'

She looks amazing, shorn like that; large green eyes and milky white skin. I had not noticed how delicate her face was before. I get out of bed and lean down to run my hand over the sandpaper stubble.

'Don't let your head burn,' I say. 'I suppose you're a sun block baby?'

Ruby nods. 'Slip, slop, slap.'

*

Ruby takes a Valium as soon as we get to the airport, and the levity of this morning is gone. 'I was bad enough about flying before half the airport was blown up. Now…' She shakes her head in distress. 'I'm sure that's why I got so stoned last night. So I could get some sleep.' She looks drawn, her pupils are dilated. Her movements are jerky. 'Doesn't it scare you?'

'It makes me horny, I'm afraid.'

'That's insane,' she is trying to make a joke but just sounds abrupt. 'You're nuts.'

We stand in a long queue for the security check and she shuffles nervously, shifting her weight from one foot to the other. 'I'm going to flip. You'll never talk to me again.'

'I will,' I say. Then I pass her a piece of white quartz I found years ago on a beach in Oregon. 'Take this stone. It's my travelling talisman, it will keep you safe.'

As we file onto the plane she grips my hand. Her anxiety is infectious, especially when it becomes clear that there is, actually, a problem. Someone has checked their bags then not got on the flight, so all the bags have to be taken out of the hold then put back in again. The plane sits on the tarmac for an hour and a half and the aircondition-ing isn't on. The heat and stench become unbearable.

'I told you. I told you things would go wrong.' This isn't the Ruby I know. All twisted and turned in on herself. 'I'm scared. It will crash. I know it. I feel it in my bones. This bag thing is a bad sign.'

'Instinct can be wrong,' I say. 'Your bones are wrong.' And I, of all people, know that to be true.

When the plane finally takes off she hyperventilates then starts scratching at her face. I grab her hands and hold them, to stop her hurting herself. 'I can't do this,' she says, 'I can't.' Then tries to get up, as if she could get off the plane.

I pull her down. 'Breathe,' I say.

'Fuck,' she bangs her head into the seat in front of her. 'I hate this.'

'Look at me. Look into my eyes.' I hold her arms tightly, look at her. 'I will not let anything happen to you. I will look after you. I promise you everything will be okay.'

'Talk to me,' Ruby says gripping on to me hard enough to make bruises.

'Okay,' I say, 'the weather: did you know that 75 billion tonnes of rain clouds cross the South Indian coastline around this time each year?'

'I didn't know that, no,' Ruby says.

'Only a third of it falls as rain,' I go on, 'and the rain that falls and makes it back to the ocean is swept along by currents from one continent to another. It turns into clouds over the desert in the USA a year or so after it has fallen as rain. The very same water.'

'Cool,' Ruby nods, but she's faking her interest. She doesn't relax until I point out the window, thirty minutes later, and say, 'There it is.'

India. The mountainous ruck of the Ghats splits the

bottom of the continent in two. There are more coconut palms than I had ever imagined possible, with the spires of churches spotted among them.

Ruby sighs with relief. 'It's almost over.'

'We're arriving,' I say. 'It is just beginning.'

In 1992, just after the first Rodney King verdict came down, I started to work for a travel agency. There was only one newspaper worth working for in Melbourne and after a few years there I applied for work as a media and marketing consultant for a company called Freedom Travel. I could think of nothing better than going to work every day and being surrounded by maps, photos and talk of other places. I'd been employed to work on the 'big picture', whatever that meant, but for the first few months I just wrote copy for brochures. It was a job that allowed me to travel, constantly, inside my head.

The Pamirs form the mountainous hub of central Asia, I might write. *They are a rugged and remote wilderness region of jagged ridges, alpine lakes and distant snow-capped peaks that stretch and fold towards the Hindu Kush and Karakoram. Enjoy a trek in these impressive mountains, spend time in the fabled Silk Road oasis cities of Tashkent, Samarkand and Bukhara. Rediscover the child that loved* Arabian Nights.

*

Not long after I started working there I had to fill in on the front desk for a day. A woman came in just as we were about to close. 'Hi,' she sat down in front of me. 'I want to go to Paris,' she said. 'On the cheap.' She peered at me. 'I want to go with my new boyfriend, Raff, he works around the corner in Readings bookstore, do you know him?' I shook my head. 'Are you the girl I talked to last time, when I was going to Africa?' I shook my head again. 'Because that was a fucking disaster, I can tell you,' before throwing her head back and hooting with laughter.

The woman's name was Marion. She was curvy in a va-va-voom way, with long black hair. The glamorous effect of this was undercut by her permanently perplexed expression—she was short sighted. Two hours later we were still talking. Friday afternoon drinks among the rest of the staff had started at some point and we sat there drinking as Marion regaled me with tales of a safari gone wrong, fading colonial towns and the increasingly heated rows with her now ex-boyfriend. Things had come to a head when a lion chased them and both headed for the same tree.

'He got there first,' said Marion, 'and was climbing up as quickly as he could. It was just a little tree. The kind you see in cartoons, the kind that bends over to the ground and places you gently into the jaws of whatever it was you were escaping from. And George—let's call him George of the jungle—could tell the tree wouldn't carry both of us, so he started flailing at me, kicking out with these massive Timberland hikers and swearing at me in a freaked-out girly voice. He came very close to kicking my glasses off.' She looked at me, deadpan. 'Anyway that's when I had an inkling that things weren't going to work out.'

Three months later Marion and I had moved in together with Raff. Marion's and my conversations together never really stopped, and once I started to become friends with Raff, he and I talked endlessly as well. They became my very best friends.

Our large terrace house overlooked acres of grey and red inner-suburban roofs and was permanently surrounded by a guard detail of stray cats. We had a bluestone lane to one side of the house, and an outside bathroom with an old door that didn't close. During Melbourne's winter we showered with the weather whipping around us. The backyard was overlooked by a huge old fig tree that filled with fruit we didn't eat and let fall onto the ground to rot.

When I was living with Marion and Raff, I started to feel I could make my little bit of the town, Fitzroy, belong to me. Slowly, I came to know the way the shadows fell down the streets on the nights when there was a bright moon, the colours of the stones and bricks, the places that offered comfort, friendship and good coffee; those where there was none to be had.

But while I loved Fitzroy, I struggled with Melbourne. It was a place with meaning hammered into the streets and the bluestones and the weatherboards: there was so much meaning I could find none. Trying to explain this to Marion, I would point through the car window when we drove places: there is the riverbank where I first kissed a boy; that is where I saw my first concert; there is the old movie theatre where I first went to a 24-hour movie marathon; over there is the street I first lived in with my mother and my dad, the same street that a large dog tore down with the blood-matted body of our rabbit in its teeth; on the corner of Punt and Bridge Roads I broke my first boyfriend's heart and he leapt out of the car while it was moving; there is the bland suburban brick veneer house where I lost my virginity; there is the street where I saw my dad walking across the road with a woman who wasn't my mother.

On the weekends Marion, Raff and I would go to the football, wandering through the autumn leaves and mud to the MCG. My family were keen Carlton supporters and from the age of five, soon after we returned from America, I would traipse off to watch Carlton play at Princes Park with Dad. He would put Finn, who was only three years old, in a baby car seat and tie it high to the wire fence at the back of the outer so Finn could get a good view.

Perhaps it was to do with loving my new dad, my passion for football. I'd recite the names of the teams to get myself to sleep at night: Carlton, Collingwood, Richmond, Essendon, North Melbourne, South Melbourne, Hawthorn, Footscray, Fitzroy, Geelong, St Kilda, Melbourne.

In 1982 South Melbourne would move to Sydney and become the Sydney Swans. By 1996 Fitzroy would be gone and Footscray would have another name. But back then I did not know that the shape of the city, the shape of everything was always changing. Back then I thought that people might come and go, but buildings, football clubs, cities: they would always stay the same.

'Why New York?' I asked Finn when I first found out he was leaving, when I was still pissed off that he was going. 'Doesn't it seem like a bit of a coincidence?'

'In what way, coincidence?' he said.

'You know, the parent split thing.'

'Yeah, right,' he said. 'I've been studying for six years so I could revisit the sacred sites of our infant traumas.'

'I didn't mean that. I know New York has things other than our family trauma going for it. And a Natural History Museum that offered to employ you. It just seems strange to me that we are both so obsessed with the place.'

'I'm not obsessed,' Finn said. 'I'm employed. You think too much.'

'You won't forget me?'

'I'm sure I will,' he said. 'But in the meantime, out of familial duty, I'll persist in making regular contact via phone and letter and the facsimile machine.'

'Fuck you.'

'No,' he said. 'Fuck you.'

We batted 'fuck yous' between us for several minutes

until we both had to collapse with laughter at our own hilariousness.

Once he moved to New York, it was I who betrayed him. I shifted my allegiance from Carlton to Geelong, Raff and Marion's team. Changing football teams is not something you should do easily, but I did, and Raff took great pleasure in seducing me away from Carlton.

'Go Cats,' he would leap, fist in the air. 'Go Cats.' Then look at me, his partner in crime, and grin. 'Lick 'em pussies.'

'You have a commitment problem,' Finn said to me in one fax, 'and I'm not sure I can call you my sister any more. You know what the great Teddy Whitten said? "Football isn't a matter of life and death. It's more important than that." Apart from which, barracking for Geelong is like going out with someone who you know is going to disappoint you. You are destined for a life of suffering.'

History would prove Finn right, but not that year. Geelong was the highest-scoring team in the competition, and they kicked 239 points in a single match—the highest score ever. 'We have God on our side,' I gloated, electronically, to Finn. 'Otherwise known as Ablett.'

'Choose your gods carefully,' was Finn's elliptical, faxed, advice.

'*Quelle embarrassment*,' I groaned one night as we were watching TV. 'That's our latest ad.' That's *my* latest ad, I nearly said, and despite my coyness I was excited by my new job liaising with the agency that produced the Freedom Travel campaign.

Marion and Raff looked up. The images were grainy, sepia. A gorgeous young guy with a five o'clock shadow and white singlet hitch-hikes down a road. It is hard to place where he is, it could be outback Australia. He turns and looks at the camera. 'Freedom. You can't put a price on it,' and the shot pans out and spins to reveal Monument Valley in the background. Then the voiceover: 'Freedom. We bring you the world.'

They both clapped uproariously when the ad was over.

'There's a whole series of these,' I said. 'All young spunks who appear to be mooching around somewhere in Australia, and then you realise they are in Japan, India, Indonesia, the States, wherever. And here's the payoff— I'm going to work in LA for a few weeks, helping to organise a mini-conference to develop our global marketing campaign.'

'I am a marketing goddess,' I faxed Finn. 'Which means I'll be coming your way soon.'

Finn sent me a fax that had a large diagram at the bottom of it: 'Dear Cath, you will see I have done a graph using my new software program to assess your current yuppiness and the rate of likely yuppiness increase over the next decade. I have also measured my own studiousness and ethical sensibility. The result of this data suggests the following: I win. PS. Come and visit me in NY when you are done in LA.'

*

The night before I went away Marion cooked a feast of curries. 'You won't be getting food like this for a while,' she said, as she served us. Then, when she had sat down. 'Here's a game. A very LA game. In the movie of your life, who would play you? Raff? You first.'

Raff had played before and had his answer down pat. 'Robert Mitchum,' he said.

'You wish,' I said. 'And you, Marion?'

'For looks I'd have to say Ali McGraw,' she said. 'But I don't think her performances have enough subtlety to capture my true essence.'

'I'd like to think I was a young Jane Fonda,' I say. 'From the *Klute* era. With a touch of *Barbarella*.'

At the end of the night Raff gave me a present. The lawn in the backyard had been wild and unruly before he mowed it into a circle. The grass around the circumference was still feet high and the boundary of the circle was surrounded with tea light candles that flickered a warm, golden light. After dinner Raff blindfolded me and took my hand.

'Come here,' he said, leading me outside and untying the blindfold when I got there. 'You stand inside it and make a wish. That's your going-away present.'

The gesture was romantic; it put me in a romantic mood. I stepped into the circle. I wish, I thought to myself, to meet the man of my dreams.

Five

'Do you know,' Ruby says, 'that Bill Gates thinks the South Indians are the second smartest people in the world?'

'Who's first?' I ask.

'The Chinese.' She laughs. 'He is a man with his eye on the global market.' We are driving down to Poovar Island and India flickers by through the car windows. I cannot understand why it took me so long to return.

Kerala is a Communist state, and hammer-and-sickles are painted on the sides of people's houses. The locals wear white to fend off the heat. The coconut palms are so thick that the light is filtered to a greeny-gold. There are Christian churches scattered at regular intervals through the trees as well as temples and the occasional mosque.

Everyone warned me that India would be more crowded, more polluted and more of a hassle since I was here last. But at this moment it seems utterly perfect. We catch a low wooden boat through the waterways to our hotel. There are fireflies darting about, and the glow of lamps from the villages scattered among the trees. It is hard to believe there is solid land in under there. In the twilight it seems that the trees are floating, that the water extends forever.

After we unpack and have dinner, we go for a walk along the beach. It is a narrow strip of sand, with the sea on one side and a lagoon on the other and there are brightly painted fishing boats beached for the night above the water line. The sea is full of phosphorescence and the surf is wild, making a continual play of fireworks, a constant sprinkling of stars.

'They are living creatures, you know, that are glowing like that. They light up when they're disturbed. Look.' Ruby runs down the beach a few metres, landing as heavily as she can on each foot, shooting stars into the air.

'You have diamonds on the soles of your shoes.'

'I love that album. You see, just because there is an age difference doesn't mean we can't like the same music.'

'On that subject, don't feel obliged to hang out with me while we're here,' I say. 'Full moon is coming. Keralan beaches are famous for their raves. I don't want to cramp your style.'

'You won't,' Ruby says. 'I might just disappear at any time. But I'm trying to be a good girl. I haven't been so into the drug thing since I had a bad reaction to the anti-malarials I was on. I had like five anxiety attacks a day and couldn't stop crying. It was foul. And let's not mention the very recent head-shaving-on-hash incident.' She runs her hand over her scalp. 'Anyway, I like being with you.'

With her clothes on and no hair, Ruby looks like a boy. But now that she is in her bathers I cannot miss her curves. Her curves—and mine, I suppose—are the reason we are sunbaking on a secluded section of sand out of sight of the fishermen. We don't want to offend them with our uncoveredness.

'I don't usually travel like this,' Ruby says, her voice muffled because she is lying on her stomach with her head cocked into the crook of her elbow. 'Normally I spend time with the locals. Work with them, if it's possible.'

'I've come to accept that I'm fooling myself if I think I can be anything other than a tourist,' I say. 'That's one of the things I like about America. I can work with people, live there. I don't feel like such a voyeur. Here, it's more complicated.'

'You're being defeatist,' Ruby says. 'You sound like my mother. It's not as hard to engage as you make out.'

'Well you sound like a naïve rebellious daughter.' I'm sharp with her. Her certainty about the world, about what's right and wrong with it, suddenly irritates me. 'But I'm glad you think you've got it all sorted.'

I've upset her, which I suppose is what I wanted. She gets up and walks down to the water without looking at me. She spends some time there, pottering in the shallows because the rip is so strong.

I get up too and move under the palms to get some shade. Ruby joins me there.

'You know,' she says, 'this heat is bringing back a memory, the first really scary thing I can remember: Ash Wednesday. Not so much the fires as the build-up. The dust storm. Did you live in Melbourne then?'

'I was in Bali,' I tell her. 'I was with my brother Finn and the day we were leaving to fly home was February 14, 1983. I remember the guy serving us in the bar saying, "Your country is on fire." We didn't believe him, but the next morning, when we were coming in to land at Melbourne airport, the air was thick with smoke.'

'I was only five,' Ruby says. 'I can remember my dad calling from work and saying we had to close all the windows because a lot of dust was blowing towards us. He asked to speak to Mum and I was suddenly scared, spooked by the urgency in his voice. I remember that more vividly than the storm itself. Later Dad told us about friends of his that stood in their driveway at Mount Macedon with wet towels over their heads while their home burnt down around them, waiting for the flames to claim them as well. And a woman who put all her possessions in a boat in a dam, only to have the fire pass over the house and burn the boat, destroying everything that was precious to her.'

'I only heard the details when we got to the airport.

The dust storm was over by then but my parents told us it dumped a thousand tonnes of sand on the city in a single hour. They told us what it was like when the smoke rolled over the city, and the stories they'd read in the papers or heard from friends. All the firemen who got burnt in their trucks as they were trying to escape from the fire front.

'Then, whenever I turned on the radio over the next few days there was the voice of the journalist who reported on the burning of his own house. His broadcast was replayed again and again, you know the way they do—*I'm watching my house burn down. I'm sitting out on the road in front of my own house where I've lived for thirteen or fourteen years and it's going down in front of me. And the flames are in the roof and...Oh, God damn it. It's just beyond belief...my own house. And everything around it is black. There are fires burning all around me. All around me.*'

'You remember what he said?' Ruby asks, 'word for word?'

'It's a grid thing.'

When I got back from the States my contact with Michael was erratic. A few days after my return to Melbourne I was still flushed with him. I sent him a long fax full of excitement about our time together. I said, 'I am pleased we have met. I think we are going to know each other a long time.'

His reply was brief. 'Know each other a long time? I'm not sure about that. I can assure you, I'm not worth it.' When I read that, standing by the fax machine at work, I flinched. I felt as if I had been slapped in the face. I got it wrong, I thought, blushing with the shame of presumption. I am an idiot.

I did not fax or write or phone—all the things I had been planning to do as I had flown the twelve hours from LA to Melbourne. But complete withdrawal was not what Michael wanted either, it seemed, and after a few weeks he began to send me postcards and brief faxes. They were so affectionate I began to believe that his rudeness had been a misunderstanding and I started to send him postcards in return. I would search out increasingly ridiculous images of talking koalas, kangaroos and girls in seventies bikinis. I wooed him with kitsch.

'It's not like we're in a relationship,' I said to Marion. 'It's not like I'm ever going to see him again, despite the occasional postcard. Sometimes I wonder if it wasn't Los Angeles that swept me off my feet. The romance of Hollywood.'

'Well if you've fallen for the myth, he must've too,' said Marion. 'He's the one living there. Anyway you will see him again. He comes back to Australia every year.'

That night I got out a video of *Legends of the Fall* and forced Marion and Raff to watch it. 'You know this is crap, right?' Raff said ten minutes into the film, having seen enough fur coats, bears and men with long hair to get nervous.

'I think it's good,' I protested. 'This is the third time I've seen it.'

'Sometimes,' Raff said, 'I have serious concerns about your judgment.'

The second time I was with Michael it was very hot. It was the summer of 1994 and fires were raging everywhere. He was home for the Christmas holidays so I decided to go up to Sydney. The first night I was there I planned to go to a homecoming party Michael was throwing even though I had not, despite receiving a postcard only a few days earlier, been invited. In fact Michael hadn't even told me he was returning to Sydney for the holidays.

'It's a dubious situation, Cath,' Marion said. 'I know I told you he would be coming back. But he hasn't told you. That's not good.'

Raff was blunter. 'He's fucking you around.'

'I like a challenge,' I said. 'I think of him as a kind of Bermuda Triangle for women.' I was laughing, but Marion and Raff were not.

'Sounds like that game we used to play in primary school,' Raff was sarcastic. 'Would you rather hang yourself, shoot yourself, or drown?'

'Drown,' I smirked, ignoring the warning in his heavy-handed irony. 'It works in with the Bermuda metaphor.'

*

I got to the party late, hoping to suggest I felt casual about it. I knew a lot of people there and spoke to them as I worked my way through the crowd to Michael. When I looked at him it hurt, I felt him in my whole body. This is what is hard to explain to people—how physical my response to him was. All I could think of was his skin and how I could get it close to mine.

Whenever I glanced up from a conversation he was watching me, his eyes upon me. But whenever I went to approach him he seemed to slip away into another room. His technique was hypnotically simple: interested, inattentive, present, absent.

As I was about to give up and leave the party Michael came out to me. 'I've been looking for you,' he said. 'If I'd known you'd be in Sydney I'd have asked you to come along myself. Do you have to go so soon? I can't leave, I have to clean up.'

'I'll be here a few days,' I said. 'Call me.'

He called first thing the next morning and came over to the flat I was staying in. He stood in the doorway of the living room, arms stretched up, hanging off the jamb. He was still lean and lined and, to me, sexy. It had only been eight months.

'Are you seeing anyone?' he asked.

'No,' I said. 'I assume you are. Is that why didn't you tell me you were coming out?'

'Not at all. I thought a girl like you would have a lot of

options and I'd be down low on the list,' he was cocky now. 'I've sent you a few postcards, haven't I? I'm hoping that will count for something.'

'It takes more than that,' I lied. 'And I want you to know I don't send bum titty bum bum postcards to just anyone. Have you got time to go out for breakfast?' I was anxious to get him out of the flat. All I wanted to do was touch him but it seemed to me that was a bad idea. I wanted to see if there was something real between us, something that sex couldn't cover up.

'Of course,' Michael looked disappointed but was gracious. 'Coffee would be good.'

Being with him in a public place just made things worse. I could barely concentrate on the menu, or the view of Bondi Beach. Michael seemed in the same state. He was shaking. Our hands brushed against each other as we reached out for our coffees and it was like an electric current ran between us. Finally, after what seemed like hours, but was probably only ten minutes, Michael reached across the table and tentatively stroked the inside of my wrist with his forefinger.

'Catherine,' he said, 'I…Could…I still feel the same about you. I didn't know that I would, but sitting here, it's driving me crazy.' His voice was quavering.

'So it's not just me?' I asked, and he grinned.

'It's not. It's me too. It's us.'

We walked home holding hands and kissed as soon as we got back in the door. We kissed, nothing else, for a very long time. I drank him, I was drunk with him. I was full of feeling and empty of it at the same time. I looked at the clock to find an hour had passed and we were still standing in the hallway with our arms wrapped around each other.

'That's to make up for missing all that foreplay in our mad desert fucks,' Michael stroked my cheek. 'But now, now I want to get dirty.'

We undressed each other slowly; I felt that I was floating. By the time he was inside me I was outside myself. This is what I need to say, again, to try and explain all that happened: no one else had ever made me feel like this. No one. When I was with him, all thought stopped. I cannot remember what we did, or what we said, only that hours passed and I was in a state that I think must have been ecstasy.

You are my church, I thought to myself, but didn't say. I knew how strange it would have sounded; the thought itself felt strange but how else to explain the feeling between us? I chased this moment, precisely this feeling, for the next six years. Michael looked into my eyes. He said, 'You have no idea how often I have thought of you. I toss and turn, you lose me sleep.'

Despite the heat, we made love all that day and into the night. After the hours of gentle we became rough. He hurt me like I wanted to be hurt. I was swollen and sore but this just made everything more beautiful.

'We should get up and get something to eat,' Michael

said, after dark had fallen. So we did. We ventured into the night to buy some Thai takeaway and some cold beers. We ate in bed and I can't remember falling asleep, but I did, heavily, and I didn't wake until morning.

Michael was stretching. When he saw I was awake he said, 'I think that might be the best night's sleep I've had in a decade.' Before I could answer I realised I was bleeding, though I wasn't due.

'Shit,' I said. 'I've destroyed Rebecca's sheets.'

Michael laughed. 'Won't you be their favourite house guest,' he said, before kissing me on the forehead and getting out of bed. 'I've got family stuff to do,' he said. 'But I'll see you tonight.' He paused. 'I mean, if you're around. If you want to.'

'Both,' I said. 'I want and I'm around.'

My friend Tony rang me when he heard I was in town. 'A few of us are going to the movies,' he said. 'Join us?'

'Maybe,' I said. 'I'll meet you there.' But I never turned up. I was waiting for Michael to call, which he eventually did, around nine that night, asking me if I felt like dinner. I said yes despite the fact I'd already eaten.

Tony called again the next morning. 'Where were you last night? Waiting by the phone?'

'I was tired.'

'So you were. Waiting, I mean.'

'No,' I lied.

I lied a lot over the next few days. I only had time for

Michael, for the idea of him. I stood up friends, cancelled arrangements at the last minute. I hung around a flat that was not my own. I waited for him to have a moment to drop by. For the rest of the time I was in Sydney, I didn't go anywhere, do anything with anyone other than Michael.

In his absence I spent my time in Bondi, falling in love with that place. One day I went to the beach and there was a flotilla of bluebottles, thousands and thousands of them, floating in to shore. They were bright and shiny blue, so pretty it was hard to imagine they were dangerous. I'd had one brand me down my thigh the first day I swam there, a line of scarred skin that bubbled and itched for the next six months. Later, one wrapped itself around my wrist when I was paddling my surfboard and I had to pick the tail off delicately, fighting my instinct to panic and brush the sting and its poison across me.

Each night Michael would arrive later and later for our date. One hour, two hours, three, and I'd sit on the balcony, waiting, looking out over the water. When he did arrive he would often talk to me about Sydney, how beautiful it was, how much he missed it. Other times we wouldn't talk much at all, he would come over and walk straight into my bedroom. It was always hot, it was always humid and I would lean over the windowsill into the evening air while he held me by the hips and fucked me.

As the fires got closer to Sydney the air became thicker. We would wake up in the middle of the night, coughing in a smoky room. There were two hundred fires burning around New South Wales; it was as if everything was swimming in a sea of smoke. Each night on the news there were fire stories and, one night, a shot of a reporter in the centre of town gesturing to the fiery suburbs behind him with a broad sweep of the arm. Houses were burning; the city was ringed by fires. A man in a torn, blackened singlet was filmed in front of the wreckage of his house. He shrugged.

'Everything is ash,' he said.

There were stories of heroes, of fifteen thousand fire fighters from New South Wales and volunteers pouring in from around Australia. Of people abandoning their cars on the highway. Of a family pet exploding into a ball of flame as it tried to escape. Of fire cutting people off so they couldn't drive out backwards or forwards. People in outer suburbs started to clear their gardens of dead wood, clear the land around their houses and hose everything down. They stood on their roofs with their hoses; waving them at the flames as if they could shoot the fire, kill it dead. Five houses in a Sydney street burnt down and the tabloids went crazy, running photos of the charred remains of a little girl's Christmas presents on the front page.

'It's Christmas,' the people who had lost everything said on the news. 'Things like this shouldn't happen at Christmas.'

But things like this always happen at Christmas. I thought of my friends whose father had walked out on them on Christmas Eve. Remembered getting up to fetch the newspaper on Boxing Day when I was a little girl and seeing the photo of a city, Darwin, obliterated by a cyclone. The stories of people's legs guillotined by flying iron; of a nursing mother being blown out of her house into the yard and crawling, on her hands and knees over broken glass, to find her newborn wedged under the front tyre of a car; of a couple and their cat jammed in a cupboard for five hours as shards of glass formed a mini-tornado inside their house, turning it into a giant blender. Christmas, I thought, is exactly the time of year shit like this happens.

The heat over those days was oppressive. Whenever we had sex we would drip with sweat, the smell of each other was strong. Michael would lift me up; we would fuck on the couch, on the kitchen bench, on the floor. He would talk while we were doing it but once our bodies were apart he said little, and what he did say was meant to hose me down, to deny the intensity between us.

'This is not a good idea,' he might say. 'I'll be leaving in a week or so.' Or, 'I have to go soon. You know what it's like when you are only in a place for a short time. So many people to catch up with.'

He talked a lot about moving back. Maybe he would, maybe he wouldn't. 'If only I could get a job here as good as the one I have at UCLA, I'd move back in a flash,' he might say. 'And you are here.' Or, 'I could never move back. Too much history. In LA I'm free of all that.'

One morning he rang me and said, 'I won't be able to see you today. It's the fires. They're getting close to my uncle's house.' That night the fires turned the full moon red. It seemed to me that the moon was always full when Michael was around—that it would be hot, that I would bleed and the moon would be fat. This night it seemed the moon itself was bleeding. Other things also kept happening when Michael was around, but I found it harder to remember them: he was always late, I was always waiting; as soon as he arrived he would talk of being gone.

The next time I saw Michael we went to dinner with some friends of his. They assumed I was a friend, not a lover, and began to make jokes about the number of women he was seeing.

'How many has he got in the queue here?' one of them said to me.

'I'm probably the wrong person to ask,' I said. 'I'm in the queue.'

After a moment's awkwardness talk turned to the bushfires.

'I'm sorry about that,' Michael said later as we walked back to the flat.

'Don't be,' I said.

That night when we made love Michael talked nervously over the rhythms of our touching. 'Have you come yet? What do you want me to do? Tell me what you like. Tell me how you like it.' Michael had got so he couldn't tell the difference between using words to turn himself on and using them to keep me at bay.

'What I'd like,' said I after a few minutes, 'is for us to be quiet with each other.'

'Whatever,' he said. 'It's too hot for this anyway,' before rolling away so no part of our bodies was touching.

The two of us tossed and turned in the heat. The wind was high, fuelling the fires as well as rattling all the windows in the flat. This was a special quality Bondi had. The wind would come off the sea and rail against the windows, shaking them in their old, loose frames.

'That noise is driving me crazy.'

'Well, do something about it.' But Michael had drifted off to sleep again. I got up; rifled through my bag looking for business cards I could fold and jam between the window and the frame. An hour or so before dawn I fell asleep, but was woken by the sun around 5.30.

Michael moved back towards me. 'Let's make the best of this,' he said, 'and go for a swim.' By six o'clock we were diving in water that the wind had made broken and choppy, scattering it with foam. Michael was a strong swimmer and I watched him move through the ocean, ash raining around him like black snow. It was cool in the water, it woke me up, I couldn't maintain my bad mood. Michael swam back to me and I duck-dived underneath him a few times, leapt on his back as a wave hit him.

'What's this about?' he shook me off. 'What are you doing?'

'It's called playing.'

Michael looked at me, embarrassed. 'Oh,' he said. I wondered what it was that had happened to him that he did not know joy.

'Should I be worried about these other women that your friends were going on about?' I asked when we were back on the beach.

'No,' is all Michael said, as he towelled himself dry. And the truth was I had such a feeling of certainty about what there was between us I did not think other women were important, I did not take them into account. This is how I saw things: I was special. This is how others saw it: I was not.

I spoke to Marion on the phone. 'It doesn't worry me.'

'It should,' was all she would say.

In English novels women sit by windows, constrained by etiquette, weather, class and clothing. If they're lucky there's a bay window with a bench set into it for that very purpose: waiting. The unlucky ones stand bolt upright by the glass, hands folded before them. Me, I was a modern girl. I sat on the balcony with a beer in my hand. Michael and I had planned to go and see a new print of *The Misfits* at a cinema down the road. So, yes, I was waiting, but I was not wearing a corset. I wore a short white linen shift that hung loose on me. I enjoyed the way the sea breeze moved over my skin, cooling me down as I sweated.

Michael walked in the door, found me outside. 'Am I

too late?' he asked. 'Have we missed it?'

'No,' I said. 'But we'd better get going now.'

Before the film began, one of my ads came on: an aerial shot swung along the Great Ocean Road and around the Twelve Apostles, and then cut in a smooth arc to the craggy outcrops of Haloong Bay in Vietnam. The sweep of the camera continued over the barren outcrops of the Skelligs, off the west coast of Ireland. Trance music spun it all together. 'Freedom. Choice. It's the same thing.'

I whispered in his ear, 'That's one of mine.'

'Right,' he nodded.

'So,' I asked, standing in the foyer afterwards. 'I know what you thought of the film. What did you think of my ad?'

'It was fine,' said Michael, 'for an ad.' Then leant down and kissed me on the mouth, his hand brushing my breast. 'I suppose it's too public to make out here, huh?'

The last night I was in Sydney Michael was four hours later than he'd said he'd be. At 10 p.m. I took Tony up on his offer of a drink and a late-night swim. When I got home at one o'clock there were three messages on the answering machine from Michael, asking me where I was.

He came around early the next morning before I left for the airport. It was only eight o'clock but it was almost forty degrees. The heat. This is the main memory that will be left of that time, when I am old, when everything else is a haze.

I answered the door and tried not to react when I saw him. That physical response was always there, no matter how badly he behaved. For his part, he averted his eyes slightly. He seemed embarrassed. He started talking, quickly, before I could protest.

'I'm sorry,' he looked genuinely flustered. 'I couldn't get to a phone earlier. I rang late last night and you were out. Here, I've brought you a present.' He held a book out in front of him, cautiously, like he was unsure I would take it from him.

I did.

'Do you want a coffee?' I asked, walking down the hallway and into the kitchen, filling the kettle.

'Thanks,' he said. Then, 'I haven't got much time though.'

'Surprise me.'

Michael sat on the couch looking nervous, sipping from the mug and looking around the room. 'I'm really sorry,' he said, again. 'I'm just not good with punctualness.'

'Punctualness?' I asked. 'Is that even a word?'

I was angry, which felt a little like being horny; at any rate I'm not sure I could tell the difference. As I straddled Michael on the couch he tried to push me away.

'There isn't the time to do this properly.'

'I don't care,' I said, lifting my dress over my head.

We rolled off the couch and onto the floor, which was hard and cool, and didn't give way when Michael pushed into me. The sweat pooled under me and made a sucking sound against the boards. When we were slick with it, Michael picked me up and carried me into the bathroom, lifting me up onto the bathroom basin. He turned the cold tap on and scooped water onto my back, and in the space between our bodies. He bit my breasts, my chest. It hurt. I liked it. The bruises took weeks to fade; by the time my skin was fresh again we were in different countries.

'Is this too uncomfortable for you?' he asked.

'No,' I said, despite the awkward angle and the way the taps dug into me. But in a fleeting second of clarity I realised the physical effect he had on me, the thing I called chemical, was a bad thing. The words flashed through my head, 'You are a virus.' Then the knowledge that would have saved me was gone, disappeared by the feeling of Michael inside me, outside me.

'You're lying, darling,' he said as if he'd read my mind. He pulled out of me. 'I told you there wasn't time for this. I've got to leave.'

He kissed me on the forehead and left me there, sprawled. I sat still on the basin for a few minutes then went into the shower and stood under the cold water. When I went back into the living room I saw the book he had bought me sitting on the arm of the couch. It was *Seinlanguage* and he had written an inscription on the inside leaf. 'Here's to all the laffs we would have if we lived in the same town.'

*

I yelled, 'Happy New Year,' to Raff and Marion when I got back home. The two of them came down the hall and into my bedroom where I was putting my bags down. 'Happy New Year to you, too,' Marion put her arms around me and I gave her a big hug.

'Hi hon,' Raff leant over and kissed me on the cheek. 'We were sure you'd been burnt up, by fire or passion.'

'Both,' I smiled. 'I've buggered my shoulder carrying these bags. I need to go to the doctor.' I paused, before launching into what was really on my mind. 'Look what Michael gave me after he'd been late for about the tenth night in a row.' I threw the book on the bed. Raff picked it up and read the inscription.

'"Laffs"? Marion's right, the guy's a wanker. What did you buy him?'

'Actually, I found a beautiful old hardback of *Les Liaisons Dangereuses* but then decided it was too good for him and kept it to read myself.'

'I was joking,' said Raff. 'Why did you get him a present in the first place? You're not still interested, are you?' He looked at me. 'Jesus, you are. Women, I'll never understand them. It's the nice men like me that always get passed over.'

'What am I?' Marion threw a pillow at him. 'Dead meat?' Then turned back to me. 'Why that book?' Books were a serious matter to Marion. I knew where she was taking this. My choice had to *mean something*. 'I thought you hated the film.'

'I did,' I said. 'But Michael has written on it. And I love writing letters. So does he.'

'Ah,' said Marion. 'You are still turning you and Michael into a great romance. Are you Swann and Odette, or Jake and Lady Ashley?'

'Aim higher,' said Raff. 'We're talking Heathcliff and Cathy here.'

'Whatever. Michael would love to imagine himself as a great, tragically flawed hero. Just as long as you don't see yourself as some kind of Madame de Tourvel. She died of grief. She hesitated, a big smile on her face. 'Raff and I have something to tell you. It's important.'

Suddenly I knew. 'You're pregnant.'

Over the next day or so the pain in my shoulder became excruciating. I felt like I was falling apart at the seams. The doctor put me on painkillers and into a sling.

Michael had called to say he would visit me in Melbourne. I did not really know what I expected, and the drugs made me so out of it I felt like I didn't care. Even those intense blue eyes of his were fading in my imagination. Briefly I thought perhaps he was nothing to me now, and the feeling was a pleasure. He arrived at my house several hours late. Even when he was on my turf he had this capacity to stretch me thin, create distance.

'What's with the sling?' he asked, when he finally arrived. 'Looks kind of kinky.'

As we lay in bed he stroked the curve of my stomach,

my full breasts. 'You're like ripe fruit,' he said. 'Ready for babies. Ready to drop.' And I wondered if perhaps he meant that he wanted to be there to catch me, to break my fall.

The next morning we went for a long walk through the gardens and streets of Fitzroy. I showed Michael the places I had lived and worked. 'Brunswick Street is one of my favourite places in the world,' I said. 'I used to live in that terrace there. And my boyfriend at the time lived just around the corner, next to that pub.' We kept walking. 'Here,' I said, 'is where you get the best maple walnut ice cream in the world. But it's disgustingly rich.'

I pointed out various landmarks as we walked. Rhumbarallas café was freshly painted in greens and reds with blobby shapes hanging around the place. 'You see those kind of amoebic shapes?' I asked. 'They are spreading through the street like some kind of viral infection. There are more of them outside Polyester Records,' I pointed. 'And the nursery.'

'I like it,' said Michael. 'It's changed since last time I was here. It feels less parochial.'

'Do you see that giant hamburger hanging off the building there?' I said. 'I slept with the guy that made that.' Michael pointed at the giant doner kebab across the road. 'And what about the guy who made that?'

'No,' I laughed. 'There are only so many makers of big things a girl can sleep with. Though I must say I found the guy who designed the giant earthworm in South Gippsland very attractive. Not to mention Big Prawn man.

'Let's go to the Black Cat. You must have been here before you left for LA. It was the first real café around here.'

We went in, sat by the window and ordered a coffee. Michael looked around the café which was furnished with bits and pieces of fifties detritus. Several very old cats were lurking around, missing either a limb or an eye. There were pot plants everywhere.

'This is nice,' said Michael, 'this city. Being here with you. I could live here.'

We got back to my house in the middle of the afternoon. Michael sat on the couch and pulled me down onto his lap. 'I'm not sure I'll have time to see you again while I'm here,' he said.

'What?'

'I'll write,' he said, holding my face, kissing me on each cheek and then softly on the mouth. 'I'm sorry.'

Then he left. As he shut the door behind him I started to shake. It became harder to breathe until, panicky, I called Marion at work. 'Is there any chance of you coming home early?' I asked.

Marion was gentle with me at first, holding my hand while I sobbed. 'This shouldn't surprise you,' Marion said, smoothing my hair away from my face. 'He has other lovers. You told me that yourself. You even thought he had someone else on the go last week when you were in Sydney.'

'No one has ever made me feel the way he does,' I spoke slowly.

'On edge, strung out, needy, horny? Darling, he's fucking with your head.'

'But the sex…'

'Good sex doesn't last. And you had to wait eight months for it, so no wonder it felt good. That's probably his tactic—keep several women on the go around the globe so no one twigs to how limited his repertoire is.'

'Maybe I could get used to it,' I said. 'Maybe I could handle this.'

'Maybe you could. If you wanted to bend yourself out of shape.'

I felt better after Marion talked tough to me and made me a cup of tea. 'I have to go out again,' Marion said. 'Raff and I promised we'd meet friends for dinner. Do you want to come?'

'I'll be fine,' I said. 'I think I'd rather be alone.'

'Okay, but promise me you won't phone him.'

'I won't.'

I wasn't fine. When I was alone anxiety swamped me. I knew he was staying in St Kilda and I drove over there around midnight, pacing up and down the street trying to summon the courage to call or go in. I paced till two a.m., till only a mad woman would have thought it was okay to ring, and then phoned him from a call box across the road.

Michael came to the phone. 'You've woken everyone up,' he said.

'Can I come up?' I asked.

'No,' he said. 'I'll come down.'

We stood together in the street, not touching or talking, looking at each other. 'You can't end things so casually,' I said finally. 'This is important. We are important.'

'I don't want to be pining for someone a long way away. I've been doing it with my wife. My ex-wife. I have no intention of doing it again.' He sounded formal and awkward like he was reciting something out of habit.

'Then why have you kept in touch with me?' I asked. 'Why have you kept things going as long as you have? You could have slept with anyone while you were here. Picked someone who didn't care about you.'

'I do like you. More than like you. I like you more than anyone I have met for a long time.'

I was silent.

'Are you satisfied now?' he said.

'No.'

Michael shrugged his shoulders in frustration. 'I'm going back to bed,' he turned and walked up the stairs.

Six

We board the boat at Alappuzha, once known as Alleppey. The boat is thatched, with a covered terrace on the roof, a small living room underneath and a bedroom no bigger than a double bed. Our captain is called Hari and we have a cook who calls himself JD. They have nowhere to sleep, or eat.

'Hari and JD can eat with us,' I say.

'They won't,' Ruby says. 'We're the wrong caste, they won't want to.' These are the things I forget about India of course, when I romanticise it in my dreams. 'This is *God of Small Things* territory,' Ruby goes on. 'Have you read it? It's all about caste. Caste and love.'

I haven't read it, but I've noticed that everyone we meet tells us what caste they are, along with their names and occupations. And the resentment towards Muslims is overt. As in Sri Lanka, politics are everywhere.

We travelled down tiny waterways at Poovar, in a

small wooden boat. We could spread out our arms and touch coconut palms with our fingertips. We floated within inches of an egret perched on a palm trunk that had been twisted by sunlight till it was slung like a hammock over the water.

In contrast, this canal feels like the Keralan equivalent of the Princes Highway—wide and dirty grey-green, with factories and car ads on either side. We are floating through a state where pollution is destroying the water-ways and poverty is increasing exponentially. I try to stop worrying about these things and enjoy the fact that mani-cured rice paddies have come into view and the pace of the boat is smooth and slow. I point out the small villages to Ruby as we pass them, but then we see the villagers washing and bathing in the river and have a shameful sense of invading their privacy.

'I feel like a Memsahib, perched up here on the roof in my cane chair,' Ruby announces. 'And I'm hot. Perhaps that is why I'm finding this so depressing.'

It *is* hot up here on the roof of this floating palace. Ruby looks to me like a wilting flower. 'Would you like me to fan you with some kind of frond?' I ask.

'Yes, please. And let's play the game where the histor-ical relic is you rather than the locals. Question one: did you see the first man walk on the moon?'

I did, of course, like almost everyone my age. I was in prep school, five years old. We were all lined up to watch the landing on the TV. I can still remember the eeriness of the flickering images. The crackle and staccato of the sound. The grey surface of the moon. The slow, heavy way that the astronauts moved.

I tell Ruby that at that time, back in '69, the milk used to be delivered to our house by a man with a horse and cart. 'I would hear it coming—you know Clydesdales? The horses with enormous feet? Clip-clop, clip-clop,' I rap my knuckles on the side of the bamboo chair, 'I would hear them coming down the street. You'd have to shake the bottle to get the cream on the top all through the milk. On winter mornings there would be frosts, on the car wind-screen, on the lawn, making it crunchy to walk on.' The frosts don't happen so much now. Now it is hotter in summer and milder in winter. It makes Melbourne feel different from the city I was born in.

Ruby smiles when I talk to her of the frost; I smile too. The thought of cold weather is deeply pleasurable.

I tell her that when I was in grade one the system changed from imperial to metric. I had only been doing maths for one year the old way, but that was enough to make it stick and I've been confused ever since. It was, I say, an in-between time; but when I think about it, every moment is an in-between time, every moment stands poised between the past and the future.

We stop further along the canal to look at a Catholic church, St Mary's. It has frescos that are hundreds of years old. They are vivid with colour, unrestrained in the violence and drama with which they portray key biblical moments. I love that about this place, the way the chaos of Hinduism influences Christianity, so that floating down the river you might see a small Ganesa shrine and, a bit further along, a Jesus shrine. Both icons surrounded by incense and laden with necklaces of flower and pieces of fabric.

It is only when we slip out of the river into Lake Vembanad that we see how beautiful this place really is. The lime factories that have lined the river shore and spread a ghostly white over buildings and trees fade into the horizon. There are pretty pink flowers everywhere, though later that evening Hari tells us these flowers are caused by pollution and their leaves are choking the lake.

As dusk descends the twilight blurs everything so I feel like I'm in Kashmir again, unable to distinguish between water and sky. Ruby sits, mesmerised. Wailing floats across the water. 'Is that sound coming from the mosques?' I ask the gnarled and grumpy Hari.

Hari looks offended. 'Not Muslims. Hindus chanting. Perhaps some Christians singing their hymns. Not Muslims.'

Ruby and I smile at each other when he says this and I wonder whether we are smiling at the same thing: our craving to find the perfect moment; the absurdity of expecting it.

Two weeks after Michael left Australia in the summer of '94, I woke to the news that LA had been hit by earthquake just hours after he'd got off the plane. The front page of the paper had a photo of freeways collapsed on each other like a pack of cards. And the news that most of the major roads downtown were closed. Dozens were presumed dead and thousands injured, thousands homeless.

'Are you okay?' I faxed Michael immediately, forgetting my promise to Marion, and to myself, that I wouldn't contact him again. He faxed me straight back.

'Have you ever touched concrete that undulates like fabric, stood on floors that rolled like surf beneath you? But that isn't the worst of it. It is the aftershocks that hit every few minutes or so which are the most distressing. There have been hundreds of them since the main quake and it is only twelve hours in. They leave you chasing your coffee as it slides around the table, afraid to stand, convinced you're crazy, convinced the building is going to crumble around you. Nothing is solid.'

I was a long way away again, Michael felt safe. He kept faxing, he was romantic, he was sweet to me. I forgot the rumours about other girls in Sydney, and forgot about wandering St Kilda in the middle of the night. Remembered only that when I was with him I bled, the moon was full, fires broke out and now it seemed the earth moved underfoot: all these things I read as signs.

*

One day Marion found a fax Michael had sent me and she confronted me. 'Are you two back in touch?'

'I was worried because of the quake.'

'Just don't wake up one morning to find five years have gone by and you're still hooked. He's not real, Catherine. *You don't know him.* Nothing is more alluring than a man you make up in your head.'

'Of course he's real.'

'No he's not. He's drama and chaos. He's Los Angeles. He's good sex.' Marion stared at me in exasperation. 'You don't get it, do you? With real boyfriends you *do things*. You hang out *after* you have sex. You talk about stuff. All you've done with this guy is fuck, get a postcard or sit by the phone in a range of exotic locations. It is not a relationship.'

'You pathologise everything,' I was upset. 'This is what all that therapy has done to you. This is what this decade has done to us. No one would ever love anyone if they went around being *sensible* about things. What I feel for Michael, what he feels for me, it's…It's *romantic*. This is what romance *is*.'

'Catherine,' Marion hesitated. She seemed nervous. 'Speaking of pathology, do you think this has anything to do with…' I knew what she was getting at. 'It can skew people's antennae pretty badly. And Michael…I think he's got a nose for damage.'

'Jesus, Marion, everyone's got their seedy stories. It's so fucking nineties the way everyone excavates some minor event and turns themselves into victims. What happened to me wasn't abuse with a capital A, it's not a big deal.'

'I don't have a story like that,' Marion looked upset. 'I think the whole word should be in capitals: A. B. U. S. E. It's a huge fucking deal to have your best friend's father grope you every time you babysit. It's not about sex; it's about having to keep secrets, and feeling like you have to play up to it, and no one noticing because everyone thinks it's normal these days for teenage girls to be sexually precocious. It's awful. Really awful.'

The few friends I had told over the years had said the same thing. To me it was a fog. I couldn't see how it was connected to the person I was now, and I certainly couldn't see how it was connected to Michael.

'Look, Laura's dad never actually fucked me. He just felt me up a few times. Lots of older people tried it on me. In some ways it was kind of sexy, it made me feel powerful.'

'I don't understand why you play this down, Catherine—you play every-bloody-thing else up. There's nothing powerful about how you behave with men now. When it comes to Michael, you're like a junkie,' she took a breath. 'This is not romance,' she said carefully. 'It is madness.'

She put a glass of red wine in front of me. She, five months pregnant, was on the mineral water. 'If I wasn't pregnant this friendship would be driving me to drink,' she said. 'Let's watch TV—"Seinfeld"'s about to start. Otherwise I'll kill you and agitate the baby.'

I leaned across the couch and took Marion's hand. 'Why do you put up with me?' I asked her.

'Like you said,' she smiled at me. 'Love isn't sensible.'

Through the perfect autumn and into early winter Marion, Raff and I planned the coming of the child. I offered to move out but they both said they wanted me to stay. Or, to put it as Marion did, 'subvert the heterosexual family norm.' They asked me to come to the birth and I took the responsibility seriously, reading my Sheila Kitzinger conscientiously. I even attended the hospital pre-natal clinic with Marion. We talked about pain control, and names, and whether it was bad to dress boys in blue and girls in pink. Raff built shelves and fossicked through secondhand shops looking for a cot and other things the baby might need. Marion and I cleared out the small study and painted it, blue and yellow like the sky and the sun. I made curtains out of an Indian print with wood-blocked elephants and then painted some elephants, and the occasional goat, down low, near the floor. I did this because they reminded me of Rajasthan and *Arabian Nights* and such thoughts had always made me happy.

'But will they make Embryo happy?' asked Raff, unconvinced. Embryo was now large enough to make Marion's stomach round and smooth with a popped-out belly button.

'Well, they won't make it unhappy,' Marion reasoned.

'And perhaps they will make it wise.'

All this should have made me less interested in Michael, but it seemed to have the opposite effect. I felt a stirring of want for the things that Marion and Raff were going to have and it did not occur to me to look closer to home to find those things.

'We've just got email set up at work,' I told Marion one evening. 'It's great.'

'We've had it for a few months already,' she said. 'I get much more work done but it's addictive. I think I'll miss it when I take time off after Embryo is born.'

I soon found out what she meant. Email changed how I felt about the world. It brought me closer to my family— my father in Paris; my dad in Bangkok; my brother in New York; my mother in Adelaide. Sometimes I felt as if I personally was being globalised: stretched thin, across the world. Sometimes I felt as if I could never find all of me in the one place at the one time. So more and more the place I found myself was at my computer, imagining Michael sitting in front of his screen on the other side of the world.

When Michael and I had used faxes, the contact was irregular, once every couple of weeks or so. But soon, with email, we were up to every couple of days. Out there in cyberspace there were no gestures to read. We didn't have to see the certain turn of the body, the angling that suggests ambivalence. We emailed each other with no idea what the other was doing at the time: drinking, working, grabbing a quiet moment away from a lover, it was irrelevant. Most importantly all these words between us, the frequency and intimacy of them, made me forget how fraught things had been when he was in Sydney and Melbourne just a few months ago.

He would lose interest periodically of course. Faxes, emails, letters were unanswered, phone calls unreturned, the waiting was so intense, so exquisite that it consumed me. I pined across, masturbated to, the distance between us. Thought of that wonderful sprawling city in the soft winter light and the sea that edged it. Thought of planes cutting through the sky to be at that airport, with him, fucking in half an hour as if one year, or two, had never passed.

'What I imagine is this,' I'd write. 'I am lying on a towel on Venice beach, hot from baking in the sun. The sun on my skin fills me with heat. I am wet, I am swelling, thinking about you…'

Time wasn't as solid in this space. I would sit down for a moment and find hours had passed. I found I could write things, say things, which I lacked the courage to say or do in the flesh. Things I was embarrassed to read once I had written them.

I told Michael what I would like to do to him. I told him what I would like him to do to me. I would describe how it felt to have him slide into me after weeks—no years—apart, shocked by how easy it was, how ready I was for him. I told him I loved his cock, how big it was. I was graphic. I described the sensation as he sat on my couch, grasping my arse, moving me down onto him. The way my cunt resisted him at first and the pressure we used to push at each other until that moment when my body stopped fighting him. The release inherent in that precise moment of giving in. I would describe him licking and biting me, holding my arse and spreading it wide as I moved upon him, so he could go deeper. I told him that I wanted him in me as deep as he could go without hurting me. No, deeper, I didn't care if it hurt. I wanted it to hurt.

It was enough to make us both come as we were reading, as we were writing. If I were at work I would run to the toilet to masturbate. I couldn't, not once I got there and the reality of the office-grey toilet walls, the fake smell of pine from the room deodoriser and the neat line of toilet rolls impressed themselves upon me, but the need was urgent.

Words amazed me. The fact that they wrought such an effect. Could make people cry, and laugh, make their body swell and harden, or soften and open. I would describe how it felt to suck his cock. As I typed I could taste him in my mouth, my lips would part. I began to miss meetings at work because I was typing so hard, so furiously. I would jump when anyone came into my office.

Sometimes Michael complained that my emails were too intense. 'Perhaps if you gave me more detail, built things more slowly,' he said, 'I wouldn't come so quickly.'

Occasionally he asked me to stop. 'I am sitting here, my cock hot and hard in my hand, and you are several thousand miles away. This is driving me crazy.'

I would masturbate and describe that to Michael. The feel of my fingers, or of the vibrator, too large really, having to be worked into my body. I would describe to him the fantasies I would have while I did that to myself. 'I imagine,' I wrote, 'that you are fucking me up the arse. It is hard for you to get your cock in, we are worried it is too big, but we manage if you use a lot of lubricant, if I lie very still, not moving, and you push slowly. You have me pinned.'

'I am not sure if that is what I want to do to you,' he answered. 'If we do it like that I will not be able to see your grey eyes and that is what I first noticed about you. There is a game I would like to play. You lie on your side and read a book to me, out loud. I will stroke you for a while, then put one finger, or two, in your cunt to see where it is your attention lies, with me and my cock that is hard against you, or with the book. Let's say it's Tolstoy: *Anna Karenina*. That's a long book. You must keep reading all the while, while I stroke you, while I fuck you with my fingers. You must keep reading as I penetrate you. You get the idea, I'm sure. I want to see how long you can keep reading for, I want to wait for that moment when all you want to do is fuck, nothing else. I want that moment to take a long time to arrive, to take no time at all. Clearly, it seems, I don't know what I want. But you know what I want. You always do. You are always right.'

'I want a look,' said Raff. 'I've always thought you were a girl with literary talents.'

'Forget it,' I said. 'I can't re-read this stuff without blushing. I'm sure the computer guy from work has read some of it and you should see the way he looks at me. I can guarantee it will send you crazy with desire. You'll stare at my breasts more than you do already. Marion will get cranky.' But then Marion, despite her reservations about Michael, started nagging as well. I showed them an extract of one of my more pornographic attempts. We sat together, shoulder to shoulder in front of their computer screen, reading. Marion kept laughing out loud, but Raff went silent.

'I didn't think it was possible,' Raff announced, 'but you have finally made me blush. You're wasted in the travel industry, you could make millions writing smut like this.' He turned back to Marion. 'Have we got time for a quickie before dinner? We both know how randy those hormones are making you.'

Marion laughed. 'It's a miracle, my darling,' she answered. 'You've been out-perverted in your own home.'

There was sex, there was the weather. Michael would write of the sky with clouds or without. Of clouds, full of rain or empty of it. There had been a hot north wind in Melbourne, in Los Angeles a hot wind had come in from the desert. Storms and dying cyclones would come down from Far North Queensland to Sydney, giving the city the feel of the tropics. In Los Angeles the storms came from the west across the American plains, exhausted of rain by the time they got there, more wind than anything else. There was so much drama in the air and sea: wild winds, killer surf, storms and heat. We would always have the weather between us, the weather to talk about. Cold currents would move south from Alaska, freezing the seas at Big Sur while the seas around Bondi were heating up, as if it were on the equator, and Melbourne sweltered in forty degree heat for days and weeks on end. The warmth would bring in sharks and bluebottles along the beaches of New South Wales. Whales would swim north earlier than usual; in California they would move south late. Summer hailstorms would pelt me, while fog hung heavy over the ocean at Venice making it impossible to surf in the morning.

He might write: 'It has been hot for weeks on end. There is no relief in sight.' Or this: 'It has been raining and in this weather this city loses all its charms.' These things felt important. Expressed, perhaps, his state of mind ('it is cloudy'), or his feelings for me ('it is hot'). That he was missing me ('I envy you those tropical summer storms, the build-up then the relief. The thunder and lightning. It gets so wild there. Here, here it is always the same').

I told Michael how it had been raining constantly in Melbourne, and then again in Sydney whenever I went there for work. 'I thought Sydney was drier,' I complained, 'so how come it rains whenever I am there?'

'People always think it rains more in Melbourne but it's not true,' he said. 'Sydney's annual rainfall is 47 inches a year—twice Melbourne's.'

'My mother has a theory,' I say, 'that the weather follows me. I think perhaps it does.'

One cold winter night, Raff knocked on my door and woke me up. Told me it was time. I got up to find Marion pacing. 'It hurts,' she said, outraged.

She staggered out to the car and lay in the back seat, curling over a large cushion I'd put there for her days earlier. Raff got into the front seat and together we drove the five or so blocks to the Royal Women's Hospital. We put Marion in a wheelchair and went up to the twelfth floor.

She was in so much pain all she wanted was a hot shower. She couldn't bear having either of us near her. 'Just piss off and leave me alone,' she hissed, so Raff and I sat in the hallway, on the floor outside the bathroom, helpless, listening to Marion's groans. Sometime, around three a.m. they took Marion into the delivery room and gave her a shot of pethidine. For a while things became very quiet and still. I sat by the window, staring out over the streets of Carlton, the suburb where I'd gone to university and hung out, the place where I worked. This night as Max was being born, the moon was bright enough to bathe the street in light. Mist hung in the air and everything shone white.

After Marion had slept for an hour or so she began to enter the contractions again. I sat by her, putting a washer on her burning forehead, bringing water to her in a glass with a straw, spraying her with Evian water. She was very self-contained. A lover of cats, she was like a cat herself, drawn deep into herself. I'd look into her eyes when the contraction was building, panting in short breaths, reminding her by example how to breathe over the pain. To breathe with someone, to look at them with such a steady gaze was a revelation. It revealed to me the quiet depth, the steadiness of friendship.

Raff, who was sitting at the end of the bed with a book of sports trivia, threw out a continuous string of quiz questions. 'In what year did Bradman make 974 test runs at an average of 139.14?'

'Easy,' Marion gasped when her contraction finished. '1930.'

'And the scores were?'

'Shut up, Raff,' I wanted to kill him; I couldn't believe he was going on like this. But Marion, Marion loved him for it.

'Eight,' she said. 'Then 131, 254, 1, 334, 14, 232.' Before doubling up and raising her hand in a firm stop sign when Raff started to ask another question. He sat quietly through the next contraction while I gave her a sip of water and changed the washer on her forehead. When he could see that the pain had receded he started again. 'Who made the most runs in a three-test series?'

'Gooch,' said Marion. 'Against India in 1990. 752 runs at an average of 125.33.'

Raff moved closer to her, began stroking her brow. 'I love you,' he said.

At around six a.m. Marion's contractions began to come apace. The doctor arrived and nurses stopped telling Marion not to push and urged her to bear down. Raff and I cheered her on, yelling, as if we were at the football.

The doctor put her gloves on, 'He's coming down,' and motioned to me to move around beside her. I stood watching as Marion strained, and started straining myself in unconscious sympathy until I almost wet myself.

There was the merest glimpse—a head covered in blood that almost came out then slid back inside Marion's body. Raff was holding her shoulders; she was gripping him by the elbows.

'I can't,' Marion said. 'I can't push again.' But she could and she did, making a deep guttural moan as she bore down with the most awe-full force. I saw it again, the head almost out, then back in again and Marion, too tired to even complain, had to muster the strength to have one more go.

The doctor pulled me closer. 'He's coming, catch him,' and before I knew it he was sliding out, a blue, blue boy with a red face, into my hands. I struggled to hold on to him, so oily and slippery and me terrified I'd drop him. I lifted him over Marion's legs and put him on her belly. The sun was starting to rise and shafts of sunlight came into the room; one actually struck the boy, as if it were a nativity tableau. Marion looked down at her son; she touched him gently with a finger.

'How extraordinary,' she said.

You can't be present at the birth of a child and not see the world differently. 'Now I know,' I wrote to Michael, 'how much I want a child. I come home every night knowing that I love more than it is safe to love a child who is not your own. I feel lonely.'

I knew you shouldn't confess these kind of things to men you wanted to love you. But I imagined I was so far away that Michael would understand. I didn't think he could possibly sense that I was becoming anxious. For a child, for a lover, for things to come together.

'Babies are nice,' Michael replied. 'Give Marion my best.' That was all. Then he continued his conversation with me about Sydney. How much he missed it. He wondered as he always did whether he should return. He asked me what I thought he should do.

Between my long letters he sent short emails. Over the years I did the same thing with these emails. I read their brevity as a loaded silence, as a grave and respectful attention to my intensity. I thought they *meant something*. I assumed that when he read my letters he thought about them and about me. Michael understood, in part, what words could do. He never made promises. But he felt free to send words of longing and encouragement. 'Write me your life,' he would say. I would live to write, write what I had lived.

'When I was an adult, when I first began to travel alone, my mum and dad still lived in Melbourne,' I wrote once. 'Perhaps that is why I love airports. Even though my parents were separated they would always come to the airport to greet me, or Finn, when we came home from wherever we had been in the world. They would bring their respective new partners and would wave banners that said "Welcome Home" while wearing silly hats in an attempt to embarrass us. Mum might wear a baseball cap backwards. Her boyfriend would wear a footy beanie. My dad might wear a colourful hat with a propeller on it while his girlfriend wore a hat that would have looked perfect at the races. The family, no matter how disparate, always rallied when it came to airports and homecoming. It brought us together.'

'Catherine,' he answered. 'Family, travel, love. With you they all seem bundled together. Tell me about a man you loved so I can rile myself up with jealousy. Write me a short story.'

So I did. I wrote the story of the first time I confused a continent with a man. The first time I loaded the fragility of love with the weight of a nation.

This love affair is neat in my memory because that is what memory does. It pulls things into shape. There were maps at the beginning, maps in the middle and maps at the end.

I was in love with my geography teacher when I was at high school. In our first class together we looked at maps of the world, maps that compared the countries that had existed before the century's wars with those that existed now. I rolled the words I saw around in my mouth. 'Do you like the name Ceylon better,' I asked when he stood behind my shoulder to see how I was going, 'or Sri Lanka?'

'I'm an old romantic,' he said. 'Ceylon.' And then he leant over me and traced the shape of that country, a country that will always be the shape of a teardrop no matter what you call it. 'Maps are beautiful things,' he said to me. 'Even if they are describing the effects of warfare. Aren't they?' And I had to agree they were.

My geography teacher visited India every year. As the years went by he brought me presents from his travels: silks, incense, earrings, and, on my eighteenth birthday, a red wool dressing gown embroidered with silk dragons. 'I think we should celebrate your entry into adulthood,' he said, with a glint in his eye.

Finally, so I could be with him, I went to India. He was still in Melbourne but I felt closer to him than I ever had before. It was in India that his stories came to life. It was in India I finally understood the kind of man he was. Chaotic, friendly, a storyteller, passionate.

In Kashmir I bought a shawl that I still wear, all these years later, like a security blanket. I lived on a houseboat for ten days and sat on the deck with snow falling around, the Himalayas, reflected in Dal Lake, encircling me. I sat for hours watching the light until I could no longer tell the water from the land and sky. On another boat, far south of Kashmir, I sat out on an open deck all night, watching fishermen's lamps bobbing at sea, hundreds of little stars.

In Mysore I bought tikka powder for my forehead and I still have the little plastic containers of colour: China red, vivid blues and greens, intense orange. Piles of flowers were placed as offerings at makeshift Hindu temples on every street corner. One day, on one of those same street corners, I stepped over the dead body of a baby girl who was laid out on a rug, a box beside her tiny corpse into which people were invited to throw coins.

The moon was full in Udaipur and I sat on the hotel rooftop by the lake smoking dope under the cold light, while the dogs howled and wedding parties danced through the streets. I rode camels into the Thar Desert where the moon was new, so fragile it lit nothing, and I lay and watched Scorpio circle over me, stars inscribing the curl of its tail as it spun slowly over me through the night.

There was a lot of illness and strange things happened to my mind. I went through periods of intense fear. I lived on Masala Dosai and Sprite. I lost a lot of weight. I didn't go out for days at a time.

Beggars chased me, thrusting mangled limbs in my face. In Jaisalmer someone spiked my lassi with a hallucinogen and I was mad for days, friends turning into skeletons around me, the floor rising up to swallow me, the walls wrapping around me. But before these visions set in there was a moment when Jaisalmer, known as the golden city, actually turned gold and glowed at me; and I received its full beauty as well as that of the desert around me.

When I got back from India I went around to the geography teacher's house. He was surprised when he saw me. 'You're half the size you were when you left,' he said and I told him it had been hard being there, and that I wanted to go back.

'Show me where you went,' he asked, so I opened up his atlas and laid it out on the table. 'I landed here, in Madras,' I pointed at the spot on the map. 'Then I went here,' I trailed my finger across to Mysore, then Bangalore and Goa. 'Then I caught the steamer,' arcing my finger through the Arabian Sea to Bombay. My fingers traced the map, his fingers traced my arm and before I'd got to Rajasthan, we finally went to bed, as I'd always known we would.

Then there was a day, a year later, when he packed his guides and his maps and kissed me goodbye. He disappeared into India, for what he called his 'big adventure'. The cards and letters came often at first, and then were more intermittent. Now I only hear from him when he comes to me in dreams—like you do, Michael. He is always smiling, and his map is always open in his hands.

'I like your story,' Michael answered. 'At the risk of being hoist on my own petard, you should be writing more.

About love, about sex.'

    'Petard?' I emailed back. 'What's that?'

    Now I am older I wonder if that was the point after all, if that was the gift Michael gave me: permission.

Seven

Ruby and I sit down to eat a Keralan curry: fish and coconut milk infused with other, subtler, flavours like coriander and lime. We try and figure out what all the ingredients are as we eat, so we can repeat this back home. The taste is so delicate that all travel's frustrations slip away.

'Enough of food,' Ruby says, after a while. 'Tell me more about the boyfriend grid.'

'It has fallen into disuse in recent years.'

'A system failure?'

'Exactly. It was another of my organising principles. I'd talk about who I was going out with like I was announcing a series of monarchs. "Hawke was prime minister when the geography teacher was reigning," or more recently: "That was the time the Catholics took power: Paul Keating on one hand, Michael on the other." Then I'd genuflect and go down on one knee. Tell me about your boyfriend grid.'

'I have no such grid,' Ruby says. 'As you say—it's a flawed system.' She hesitates before she goes on, 'And if I did have a grid it would be a girlfriend grid.'

I am surprised because I hadn't thought about it. I'd just assumed. 'I'm sorry,' I say. 'I didn't know.'

'Sorry?' she asks, sarcastic. 'Why sorry? It's not cancer.' She looks at me and suddenly she's furious. She gets up to leave. 'I'm going for a walk. I know you didn't mean to be hurtful but I hate the way you looked at me just now. As if I haven't had to listen to stories of your heterosexual obsession for weeks now. As if your heterosexuality is normal when it's totally fucking nuts but I don't care because you are my friend and I love you anyway.'

I'm confused because I don't know what she saw in my face that upset her so. I felt flustered, that is all, because it changed things for me. Not how I felt about her but… something shifted. I reach out and take her arm. 'I didn't mean…'

She shakes me off, bursts into tears and walks into the night. I suddenly feel a lot older than her, which I suppose I am. I remember what it is like to be so distressed and angry but I don't know what to say that will make her feel better. I'm uncertain about words these days; uncertain as to whether they mean anything. I stay at the table and gesture for a waiter. I need a beer.

When I get to our hotel an hour later, Ruby is in bed already, reading. She is red-eyed, but smiles at me when I open the door. I go to speak but she lifts her hand.

'Don't,' she says. 'I overreacted.' Suddenly she is Barbara Stanwyck, her voice low and mysterious. 'Let us never speak of this again.'

We are in the city of Kochi, which is a series of small islands linked by ferries and bridges. It is on one of these islands, Fort Cochin, that we visit St Francis. The church is so old that no one knows when it was built. Tombstones from an early graveyard form the floor of the church. The medieval script and illustrations on the tombs are worn down to shadows, the merest suggestions in stone. Here the famous Portuguese explorer Vasco da Gama was buried but also, as I discover when I see her tiny gravestone, the unknown Bunny La Cruz. I become fascinated with Bunny. I try and imagine what she might have looked like dressed in the formal baby clothes of the sixteenth century.

'If I ever have a daughter,' I say to Ruby, 'I'd call her Bunny La Cruz.'

'Bunny La Cruz Monaghan? Sounds good. If I ever have a son I'll call him Vasco. Vasco Miller.'

We walk to Jew Town and down the bluntly named Jew Street. We hover around overpriced but irresistible antique shops, which used to be run by Jewish merchants but now are run by Kashmiri refugees. When we get to the end of the street we visit the 450-year-old synagogue. It is a small wooden building with a floor of disparate Chinese tiles and a ceiling dripping with nineteenth-century Belgian glass chandeliers.

'Now this is what I call globalisation,' Ruby says.

In the early evening we go down to see the Chinese fishing nets. They look like enormous string clams and it takes four men to open and close them. We pick fish to eat from one of the stalls and it is grilled for us while we stand there.

'Did you catch that fish here?' I ask.

'No,' the fishmonger nods his head. 'There are no big fish left here. From out deeper,' he gestures out behind the nets to the open sea.

As we are returning to our hotel a beggar puts his hand out to us. I shake my head. 'I have no change.'

He gets angry. 'You are rich,' he yells. 'Give me money.' Which is when I see the hole in his face, his caved-in nose. He has leprosy. Ruby takes my hand and we walk quickly, but he keeps pace with us, grabs our arms and tugs at our clothes. Ruby is crying by the time we get to our hotel courtyard.

'Sometimes I hate this place. I don't know how you stand it,' she looks at my tearless face accusingly. 'You are too thick skinned.'

'That's not fair. We didn't have any money, there is nothing we could have done.'

'That's because we spent it on antiques,' she jerks her laden bag towards me. 'That is because we are staying in this hotel. No wonder the guy thinks we're full of shit.'

I'm tired of this, of her, of her big emotions. I'm beginning to wonder if we should keep travelling together.

If the age difference is a problem. But I do the right thing; I lean forward to comfort her. For the second time in twenty-four hours she moves to avoid me and goes ahead of me to our room.

I give her a few minutes, and when I get to the room she is in the bathroom. She hasn't shut the door, which I take to be a gesture of forgiveness, and I watch her as she scoops the water out of the tiled tub and pours it over her head.

'You are getting goose bumps,' I say. 'I can see them from here.'

'It is nice to be cold after so much heat,' she says. 'I can't wait for the rain to begin. This build-up—it's making me so tense.' She rubs herself down with soap, seems unself-conscious about me standing there, talking to her as she scoops water between her legs, over her head and back. Suddenly she hesitates, lifts her head and smiles at me, before closing the door.

When she comes out of the bathroom she smells of jasmine oil. 'Smell this,' she says, tipping her head towards me. 'It's what the women rub into their scalps. I bought it today.' I lean down and put my face to the top of her head to breathe in the smell of jasmine. I get oil on the tip of my nose.

Geelong was in the 1994 Grand Final. I sat down to watch it with three-month-old Max draped across my chest like a large cat. He snuffled, he was heavy with abandon and as he breathed against me I fell asleep and missed the whole match. This was, as it turned out, no bad thing. Geelong was slaughtered, scoring 8.15 to West Coast's 20.23. I woke up to find Marion asleep in the chair beside me, the television off, and a note from Raff on the coffee table, 'Fuck this for a joke. Gone for a walk.'

This was a time of open fires and shared meals. I'd cook and Marion would sit in the kitchen, breastfeeding. She said less than usual, seemed too happy for words. 'I never expected it to be so good,' she said to me one evening. 'I never knew I could feel so much.'

Raff was more practical. 'I'm giving up dope,' he said to me. 'It makes me too anxious. Things are so good that I keep expecting them to go wrong.'

I knew that feeling. That feeling of not trusting happiness to last. It almost made me want to leave this house, where I had been happy for so long.

Raff took some months to forgive Geelong, so in early '95 we found ourselves going to see other teams. Around the time the Alfred P. Murrah Federal Building in Oklahoma was bombed on April 19, 1995 we went to see the first Essendon–Melbourne game at the MCG. The papers were full of photos of young children killed in the blast; also body parts of some of the other 163 who died. There were photos of Timothy McVeigh, the young man from Kingman, Arizona, in leg irons and handcuffs. The bombing happened two years to the day after the raid on Waco. Statistics. If you like football you've got to like stats.

The match was huge, more than sixty thousand people in the crowd. It was autumn, which in Melbourne usually means perfect weather but on this day it was cold, the sky a steely grey, and it was sheeting rain. Nonetheless when we got to the ground my excitement rose, as it always did, when I saw the green of the oval, the jumpers of the players and all the people within the stands spread out before me.

As charged up as I was about the match, I was having trouble concentrating. I had something to tell Raff—that I was moving to Sydney. It had taken a while, but finally I'd convinced work to transfer me there and it was only now, now that I had to break the news to my friend, that I realised I didn't really know why I was going.

When I spat it out he looked at me blankly from underneath his rain hood for a moment. 'What about us? What about Max and Marion and me?' Then he turned back to watch the game.

'Raff,' I touched his arm, but he shrugged me off.

'It's pathetic,' he said, 'moving there so you'll be closer to him. And you're going to change teams again, I know it; you'll defect to the Swans.'

'Closer to who?' I asked. 'I'm going for the beach. I'm going for the weather.'

'You know who,' he said and I realised with a shock that this hadn't occurred to me. That I might be harbouring hopes of seeing Michael more, of him moving back to Sydney.

'You're wrong,' I said, but once Raff put the thought in my mind I became terrified he was right. 'I couldn't live with you guys forever,' I said. 'I need to make something...a family. One of my own.' Raff wasn't interested in hearing this. He just shrugged again; perhaps he knew that it was more than that. The three—now four—of us had got too close. I was starting to feel claustrophobic, starting to feel like I couldn't breathe.

I was barracking for Essendon that day; the match was slow, they were losing and we were stuck sitting under an umbrella in the rain. Then, in the second quarter, Michael Long was caught holding the ball. The free kick went against him, provoking a groan of disgust, especially from a bloke sitting three rows in front of us.

'You black bastard,' he yelled. He was about fifty-five, big, clean cut and well dressed, with hair short enough at the back of his neck to see that it was, in fact, red. 'You stupid black faggot.'

Raff turned to me. 'Did you hear that?' he said. 'Did you hear the FUCKING racist in front of us?' Raising his voice to make sure the people in front could hear. The man who had been doing the taunting turned around. 'You talking to me? If you're calling me a racist I'll punch you in the fucking head.'

Raff pitched his voice lower, angry, making sure the guy had to strain to hear him. 'But you are mate, you're racist scum.'

The next thing I knew this man had leapt over three rows of chairs and, before I even had time to think about what he might be about to do, he'd done it—slammed his fist into Raff's face and sent him sprawling back in his seat. Then I was on my feet waving my own fist in the guy's face. I wanted to punch him. I wanted to hit him as hard as he'd just hit Raff, but the woman he was with grabbed his arm and dragged him away.

Raff sat down and fiddled with his mangled glasses. People were slapping him on the shoulder to see if he was all right but he wouldn't look up. He wouldn't look me in the eye. A few minutes later I peered at him and saw that there was blood running down his face from where his glasses had cut into him on the bridge of his nose. He was trembling and there were tears running down his face. I didn't know whether that was because his nose was hurting or from sheer distress.

'I'm sorry,' I said, putting my arms around him. 'That you are hurt. I am sorry people behave like that.' We leant together so our faces were touching.

Sydney is a place that gets under your skin. The way it smells, the way its moist heavy air pushes against your skin. One of my very first memories is being taken there as a tiny child and staying up late, sitting on a hill watching the lights of the racecourse, the movement of the people and the horses caught under them, going round and round. I know now I was at Harold Park in Glebe where they run the trots, but then, as a child it felt like somewhere very exotic and exciting. Warm air, and lights and movement. It was the same when I went to live there; this body-response to the place. I loved the rocky coast and harbour. Loved the weather. I was a pot plant that had finally been given enough light.

I moved in with Tony. He was a journalist with the *Sydney Morning Herald* and many years ago, when he had been one of my journalism lecturers, we'd had an affair that was truncated by one of my extended trips overseas. He had quite a strong Italian accent that he was embarrassed by; he was ambivalent about his homeland but it informed everything he did, the friends he made, the politics he wrote about. He would tell me sometimes that the rocks and colours around Bondi reminded him of Sicily.

He was recently divorced from a woman that none of us had ever liked, though we all tried to be polite about her. He needed someone to share his apartment on the tip of Ben Buckler in North Bondi. The wall of the building merged with the cliffs that plunged down into the ocean below. The wind was always wild there—at the point there was a boulder that had been dumped onto the rocks and the little metal plaque on it read: 'This rock weighing 235 tons was washed from the sea during a storm on 15th July, 1912.' Apparently two rusty mermaids used to sit perched on this rock, but they were gone by my time.

Everything I owned that was metal—my stereo, my car, my fax machine, my computer—was soon rusted by the salty air. The paint peeled and all the furniture was covered in a coating of sticky salt. Everything was permanently damp.

'That's the price you pay for living in one of the most beautiful places in the world,' Tony said. It didn't seem such a high price. I loved it there.

Tony was weathered, like the cliffs he lived on. He had curly silver hair and dark olive skin. He would swim each morning at Bondi beach and each evening at Bronte pool. Perhaps that is why he looked so fit. He'd been a champion sprinter as a schoolboy in Italy. 'For this reason,' he told me with no modesty at all, 'my thighs are very strong.' And it was true, they were like tree trunks. In contrast, his hands were tiny, they flitted around as he talked. He was less proud of these. 'Kind of poofy, huh? Or do you think they are artistic?'

To celebrate my first week in Sydney we went to have a drink at a place near where we both worked. It was a revolving cocktail bar on top of the Australia Building, once the tallest building in the city. The décor hadn't been changed since the seventies, a fact that was starting to make it fashionable again but had not, at this time, completed the process. We sat, cocktails in hand, and slowly inched our way around the sweep of the city and harbour.

'I shouldn't complain,' I said. 'My office is right in the middle of the Rocks. I get off at the station at Circular Quay, I walk past the MCA and through the Argyle Cut. That has to be one of my favourite bits of city in the world, the way the ferns grow in tufts from the cracks of those hand-made bricks.'

'They are more than 160 years old, those bricks, you know,' Tony told me.

'So it's all good. Except they hate me in my new office. One of the other workers thought she was up for my job, but instead she's working for me and giving me a hard time. My office isn't set up. I don't have furniture. The computer guy still hasn't got around to setting up my email.'

'Aahhh, that is why you're so jumpy,' said Tony. 'Email withdrawal syndrome.' He was joking, but he was right. I felt anxious without email. I had become used to the notifier flashing in front of me dozens of times a day, holding the promise of Michael.

Three days later I got to sit down at a desk, with a computer, and log on. An email from Michael greeted me. 'You've arrived! I'd welcome you home properly if only I still lived there. Enjoy and take care—M.'

The next day he emailed me again to give me the names of people I should make a point of meeting. He put me in touch with his family—his parents, his sister—and several other friends. He trusted me with people he loved, and they made me feel welcome. I liked them. Over the next few months there was a flow of invitations to birthdays, the movies, dinners. 'It is as if,' I wrote to Michael, 'I have become the sister-in-law, or the daughter-in-law, without having the husband. I'm not sure if this is a good thing or bad thing.'

'Trust me,' he answered. 'You're getting the best part of the bargain.'

What I didn't say to him was that his family's kindness entangled him and me further. Nor did I say that Raff had been right. It seemed that in moving to Sydney I had moved closer to Michael, just as I had come to know my geography teacher by going to India. Sydney was where he had lived, and grown up. Everybody knew him. He no longer seemed so far away.

There was also the Sydney I discovered with Tony. 'The only way to really know this city,' he said to me soon after I arrived, 'is to kayak. I've got a five-week plan for you. We'll paddle around Middle Harbour and Pittwater. A different kayak trip every Sunday.'

I agreed to the plan. The mildness of Sydney's weather meant you didn't have to put on a wetsuit, like you did when you kayaked in Victoria. We would put on our rashies—Tony's was black and mine was blue—and smother our faces in fifteen plus, put on baseball caps and sunglasses and off we'd go. By Melbourne standards we looked like dorks. In Sydney, dagginess resulting from sporting paraphernalia was more acceptable.

That first weekend we paddled around the edges of Middle Harbour and Tony, an enthusiast when it came to architecture, pointed out all the best houses on the waterfront. Another weekend we went to Pittwater and, despite the wildness of the coves and beaches, we found ourselves at sea with hundreds of other boats, including one that sold us lattes and good muffins.

Sydney has this great ability to appear, in all its glorious cliché, more beautiful than you can imagine, and that physical beauty becomes addictive. One day we pushed out from Watsons Bay and headed for the national park that fell, blooming and green, onto the beach at Obelisk Bay. The sea was calm and the water sparkling.

'Be careful,' Tony warned me. 'All the rain this week has forced raw sewage into the harbour. It might still look gorgeous but just make sure you don't fall in.'

The harbour had a particular kind of beauty, Bondi had another. It was a place where informality had been ritualised. People never arranged to meet. When the weather was warm, which it was until close to winter, they simply hung around their chosen bits of the beach and waited for others to show up. I met lots of people like that. Vague acquaintances who, over the weeks of morning swims, coffees and walks, became friends. It was a bit like Venice beach, or Venice beach was a bit like it. Lots of flesh and sun and sand and parading. The weather shapes your day in both places, you have to give yourself over to it, though the weather got wilder in Bondi. And while Sydney was a large and difficult city, Bondi, if you learnt to move around the constant stream of visitors, was like a village. I didn't interact with the tourists and talked about them with the same disdain that all the locals did, but their presence made Bondi the perfect suburb for someone like me who always liked to imagine they were living in other places.

Every morning when I went down to the beach to walk and to swim, buses full of Japanese and American tourists would be lined up. I'd watch them removing their shoes, feeling the sand between their toes, taking photos of each other. When I went overseas myself everyone I met knew Bondi, had seen the photos of this crescent moon of beach—the beach, and its famous surf. But I loved it best when the water was as flat as a mirror and I could swim, seeing clear to the ocean bed that was laid out below and before me.

Dolphins surfed the waves in the morning, playing with the surfers, while people watched from the beach and smiled and nodded at each other. One morning Tony and I were sitting out the front of a café that overlooked the water.

'Does my nose look big?' he asked. It had become a running gag—his nose was huge and he thought it was ugly. He would say to me, 'It makes me look so Italian,' and I'd say to him, 'You are Italian. I think it's sexy.' Then he would say, 'Do you really?' and smile; like it was the first time I had said it.

It was a warm winter's day and half a dozen Bondi-ites sat in their dark glasses and Mambo tracksuits reading the papers. I turned to look out at the ocean and there, fifty feet away, a whale was rolling lazily, holding its flipper aloft. I had never seen a whale before though I'd spent various holidays over the years on rocky outcrops with binoculars in my hands, jumping at every shadowy shape in the distance, every smudge on the horizon.

'You see,' Tony leant towards me. 'There is everything you could possibly want, right here, in this suburb. That is why people never leave.'

On warm nights, Tony and I would take a drink down to the beach, just before we went to bed. In early summer the water was at its coldest because winter caught up with it three months after the season itself ended. As far as I was concerned, that just made it more exhilarating. One night the surf was high and I decided to swim out to catch a wave. Tony stood on the beach, yelling at me.

'Do you have any idea how many pissed tourists die each year doing what you're doing?'

'I'm prepared to risk it.'

'Well I'm going back to sit in my car and put the head-lights on. Promise me you won't move out of the spotlight.' He walked up to his car and put his lights on high beam while I attempted to bodysurf. 'Stay in the lights,' he kept calling, which was impossible, as the beam dropped into the water about two feet from the shore.

'I'll die of sand rash, not drowning, if you keep carrying on like this,' I yelled.

'I can't take it any more,' Tony yelled back before he jogged back down to the beach, then dived into the water and swam out to me. When he got to me he manoeuvred me, half-joking, half-seriously, into a lifesaver's grip, then started to sidestroke me back to shore.

I couldn't stop laughing. 'You remind me of a sheep dog,' I said. 'Always trying to round me up.'

'And you remind me of a sheep,' he said. 'A wet one.'

I didn't think about what was happening with Tony, about the time we spent together, the comfort I felt around him. It just made sense to me that, as the nights got hotter, we did what housemates sometimes do, what ex-lovers often do. We would lie in bed and talk until the small hours of the morning. And as we talked we would touch each other, and sometimes the touching would turn to sex. There was a sweetness to our times together, but I would always go back to my bedroom for a few hours of sleep. We never woke up together.

One night it was different. We'd been to a friend's birthday party on a Bondi rooftop. It was a hot, sticky night and we'd danced with, and talked to, each other all evening. I was touched by the shy way he danced, by the fact he was dancing to be close to me, not to show off to other people. We kissed in public at the end of a sexy dance to, embarrassingly, 'Sexual Healing'. Now questions would be asked.

We left the party early to make love. That was hot and sexy and slow as well, like the whole evening. 'Do we need to talk about this?' I asked afterwards, after the sex was over. 'This seems to be becoming a weekly not a monthly event.'

'I don't need to talk,' he said, 'I'm happy. Do you? Need to talk, I mean.'

'I'm not good at casual,' I said. 'But I'm not available either, so I don't know what to do.' As the words came out of my mouth, I realised what I'd said.

'Not available?' Tony still had his arms around me, but I could feel his tension. 'I didn't know you were seeing someone.'

'I'm not,' I said. 'Well I am. But he's overseas.'

'That Michael guy? You haven't seen him for over a year and he's not even calling himself your boyfriend.'

'It doesn't make sense. I know that.' Now I was tense. I got up, ready to go to my own room.

Tony grabbed me, pulled me back and put his arm around me. 'It's fine,' he said. 'I was just surprised. But I'm still fretting over the evil Julia, so I'm not really available either.'

'So,' I hesitated. 'Fuck buddies?'

'I hate that phrase,' Tony said. 'It's disgusting. This is how I see us. Like two planes circling beside each other waiting to land. We are doing the same thing at the moment but perhaps we are going to land in different places.' He kissed me on the forehead. 'We're airport buddies.'

*

'Sometimes I think,' I said to Tony over dinner one night a few weeks later, 'that I'm not a nice person.' I was smarting from a comment a new acquaintance had made when we had met for lunch. Intimidating, she had called me. Reserved.

'Of course you are a nice person,' he said, waving his hands around even more than usual. 'But you have edges, people injure themselves on you. You know those coffee tables at the Adelphi in Melbourne? All metal and sharp corners, and everyone who stays there damages their shins? You're like that. You sit in the centre of things in everyone's way looking shiny and gorgeous. Then you are surprised when people fall over you. You think you're the wallpaper, but you're not, you're the coffee table.'

'Ah-ha,' I said. 'Pop psychology meets interior design. Very Sydney.'

'But,' he went on, ignoring me, 'if what you are asking is whether it makes sense that you are oblivious to me because there is a chance that you might get laid by a man who lives in another country some time in the next year, I'd say no.'

'I thought we were circling planes?' I said nervously, not sure whether Tony was seriously trying to discuss our relationship or was just continuing in his generally flirtatious style. 'I didn't think you wanted more.'

'What would you say if I did?'

'I don't know,' I said. 'Good? I think.' And as I said it

I meant it. Michael was becoming a blur; it was Tony who was coming into focus.

'Well, if we are still enjoying each other's company come Christmas time, why don't we go away for a week or two? To Byron Bay.'

'It's a deal,' I said.

Michael's sixth sense was up and running and the next day an email arrived: 'What are you doing over Christmas? Going to go to New York to see Finn? Why don't you come through Los Angeles first? We could have some fun. Drive to Mexico or something.'

'I have nothing planned,' I typed, not even waiting a full minute before I answered. 'I'd like to come over.'

It took me a week to tell Tony that I had booked the flight, and even then I was evasive about it. Even worse, I brought it up when he had his back to me doing the dishes, so I didn't have to look him in the eye.

'You know how we talked about Byron over Christmas? I have to go to New York for work, so I wanted to take advantage and stay on to spend Christmas with Finn.'

'Are you stopping in LA?' There was a pause. 'For work? To take advantage?'

'Yes. I mean not work. I mean…'

There was another awkward silence, then I said, 'I'm sorry; it's just that I don't really know what it is between us. We're not really an item and…'

'You and Michael are,' he paused, then went on scathingly, 'an *item*?'

I said nothing.

'You're a fucking idiot,' he said, throwing his candy pink dishwashing gloves onto the kitchen bench and walking out of the room.

Eight

'These last few days have been a bit of a low point,' Ruby says. 'In more ways than one. Today, I am in charge of the itinerary.'

Despite my misgivings about continuing to travel with her we have caught a bus to Thekkady, just out of Periyar National Park. We are both being nice to each other and I'm beginning to enjoy Ruby's company again. We spent yesterday in pursuit of some of the world's last living tigers. We saw nothing, of course. Our 'Wildlife Lake Cruise' was one of half a dozen boats that set off late each afternoon. The noise of all the engines scared most animals off, though we did see some water birds, a few deer, a hyena-looking thing and some water buffalo, which, for an exhilarating moment, I thought were elephants. Our guides told us endless tales of animals being poached and killed, 'for the Chinese aphrodisiac'.

We walked at dusk, in the hope of seeing some rare

goats. There was a traffic jam in the car park and, as if in mockery of the signs that line the road requesting silence, the drivers leaned flamboyantly on their horns to hurry the traffic along. So, no goats.

'Today,' Ruby elaborates, 'we are going to the spice farm.' I am dubious, thinking it will be yet another tourist trap, but I have no better suggestions. As soon as we arrive at the farm I'm won over.

'What does this remind you of?' our guide, Neehal, asks us. He rubs a seed he has picked off a vine between his thumb and forefinger. We lean towards him and breathe in. I know the smell but can't place it, it is too subtle.

'Cardomon,' Ruby says, and is right.

Neehal bends down and digs up a small root, like a tiny piece of ginger. It is waxy skinned and pink on the outside but when he snaps it open it is chalky and an intense yellow. He takes my hand and turns it over, rubbing the root across the back of it, staining it.

'Turmeric,' he says.

We look at peppercorns, pink, black and white. He describes for us the multiplicity of ways in which the peppercorn can be prepared and when we should use each variation. We inspect the bark of a cinnamon tree and the flowers whose stamens become cloves. When we get to the pods of the cocoa plant Ruby gasps with pleasure. 'Oh my god,' she says. 'Chocolate.' I have such a moment my-self when we pass a coffee bush, manicured like a bonsai tree.

After the tour is over Neehal takes us into the small spice shop and gives us a cup of ginger tea. I sit and drink, watching Ruby running her hands over and through the spices. She brings me over bags of colours and smells. Chillies, clove, peppercorns, cinnamon, tea, ground turmeric, and tiny, expensive packets of saffron threads imported from Kashmir. As we leave the shop Ruby says, 'Neehal asked me out for a drink.'

I feel a twinge. 'Are you going?'

'No,' she says. 'I'm not sure that traditional Indian men are really on top of lesbianism, so to speak.'

Some hours later, emboldened by Ruby's talking about things lesbian earlier in the day, I decide to ask her what it's like. Lots of my friends are lesbians and I've never given it a second thought. But with Ruby, I find that I keep thinking about it, about what it is she might do. 'So are we allowed to speak of it yet?' I ask. 'Of the love that dare not speak its name?'

'Yes,' says Ruby shortly, with a slightly forced smile. 'I'll try not to go off again.'

'Okay, this is it. This is the question: what do you do with women in bed?'

There is a long silence before Ruby laughs out loud and says, 'You're an idiot. That's your question? That's what you ask when it *clearly* is a sensitive'—she draws quote marks in the air—'subject?'

'I have told you everything about me,' I push on.

'Including my sex life. You can't get out of the conversation just by being gay. That's cheating.'

'What you've told me about you is that you had super-human-pseudo-spiritual-sex and it drove you crazy. I don't think I can compete.'

'You know what?' I say. 'I'm starting to think that's the spin I need to put on things to justify the stupidity.'

'That's not how you tell it.'

'You're attempting to divert me. Details. I want them.'

'I have no idea why people find this question so fasci-nating. How's this: we kiss for hours. We lick and smell each other, we rub our bodies, our skin against each other, we bury our faces in each other's cunts, and we put fingers inside each other. And if things are going well we get our hands in too.'

I blush. 'How do you breathe? You know, when you go down on someone and your face is pushed into them?'

'Using a snorkel helps,' she says, and I wonder, for just a second, whether she is joking or not. She sees hesitation cross my face and is triumphant. 'Got you.'

'I'm easily tricked,' I say. 'For several years I couldn't eat cous cous because Finn told me it was made out of sheep's nose gristle.'

'So,' Ruby is laughing. 'Do you want me to go on with my sex talk?'

'Absolutely,' I say. 'Challenge my limited imagination.'

But she doesn't. Instead she takes from her pocket some of the cinnamon bark she has bought and rubs it between her hands and across her face and her neck, as if to wipe off the sheen of sweat that the heat has lain over her. Then she leans across the table and places the cinnamon under my nose.

'*I am the cinnamon peeler's wife,*' she quotes. '*Smell me.*'

I hadn't seen him for two years, had only been in Los Angeles for an hour and his house for ten minutes when Michael started to kiss me. I bit his lips, his throat. It was just like I had dreamed it.

'We better get you walking,' he said after we'd had sex and I, pleased to be in a bed, started to fall asleep. 'Or your jetlag will get worse.' When Michael got up he saw there was blood.

'Am I imagining it,' asked Michael as he pulled the sheets off the bed, 'or does this happen every time?'

'It does,' I said. 'Did I mention that I'm a witch?'

Michael lived in a small cottage in a compound, surrounded by a garden. His house was like a much-loved doll's house: small and pretty and perfect, but in a rundown kind of way. He looked older now, though his eyes were the same beautiful blue. He had turned fifty and it seemed to me that a certain vulnerability had beset him. Perhaps it was his age. Perhaps it was seeing him being domestic, at home. He was paler too. 'Even in California,' he said, 'it is not dignified to have a tan when you are over fifty. That doesn't stop some people, but it's stopped me.'

'You're not old,' I say. 'Not to me.'

'I feel it,' he said.

I was seriously disorientated by jetlag, more than I ever had been before, so I sat around the house, a little like a doll myself. Slept and fucked and read. Michael was busy most days; kept saying he had to work. I took melatonin that made me sleep at night, heavy and long, and left me feeling stoned.

'Watch how much of that stuff you take,' Michael smiled on the second evening. 'It makes people libidinous.'

I thought he was joking but I read later that it was true. Perhaps that was another reason we had so much sex, but whatever the reason it put me in a kind of daze. There was only desire, a kind of madness: no language. That feeling was what I called love—I loved the cottage, I loved Los Angeles, I loved Michael. In that place, I was in love.

I found I couldn't handle too much sunlight, not even the Los Angeles winter light. It was not hard and blue like you see in the movies but creamy and yellow. The sun sat at a low angle making everything slightly blurred, as if it was always dusk. I kept dropping off to sleep at odd times and on the fourth day Michael came home early in the afternoon to find me curled up on the couch.

'Hey,' he said softly, sitting beside me, kissing me on

the shoulder. 'It's still daylight. You should try and stay awake.' I sat up and kissed him on the mouth.

'That's right,' he spoke so low it was a moan, 'wake up so we can go to bed again.'

We began to make love for the third time that day. Michael sat on the bed, his back against the wall and I sat astride him. I loved fucking him this way. I could move as I wanted. His mouth could reach my breasts and his hands could cup my buttocks, lifting me, spreading me wider. It was a way I often came. But this time things were difficult. Already I was thinking that we would be apart soon, that I'd be back, in Sydney, away from him and back in my head, where I'd been stuck for years. We moved together for some time and I could feel he wanted me to come. We both were tired, and sore, so I moved increasingly faster, put my mouth against his neck and moaned, then stiffened. Michael stopped moving, held my face.

'You faked that, didn't you?' he asked. 'You don't need to do that.' He kissed me.

'No, I came,' I lied. But, caught out, I felt a small stab of triumphant intimacy; he could tell the difference between fake me and real me.

'I don't believe you,' he said, grumpy now. He rolled me over and kissed me on the collarbone before withdrawing from me.

In the evenings we would walk around Venice and Michael would tell me its history. He was a good teacher, he made things sound interesting. 'At one stage Venice was a separate city to Los Angeles,' he said. 'The idea was to improve upon the Italian Venice. Imagine, the arrogance. It was to be a fairytale city of canals floating between the sea and the desert, but by 1930 the canals were full of silt. The gondoliers were being sent back home to Italy. The Americans are nuts sometimes.'

'Perhaps they'd call it vision.'

'No doubt. It was created by a class-A nut called Abbot Kinney in 1905. His "vision" included the mass planting of eucalypts and Anglo-Saxon racial purity through eugenics; just so you know. Now to more recent history: that's the phone box where Keanu Reeves is making a phone call when the first bus blows up in *Speed*,' he said, pointing to a phone box on Main Street and Sunset Avenue.

'There,' he swung around, pointed, 'is where he got his takeaway coffee before he went to the phone box.'

I was inspired, and finally, for the first time in days, left the house on my own. I borrowed Michael's car and cruised LA like I was in my own private computer game. I got onto the Hollywood Freeway at Echo Park, which meant that I had to move left, across six lanes of traffic, and take the same exit as Keanu takes when he discovers they haven't finished building the road yet. The rush of driving there, having to do it fast, was a real buzz.

'It's silly, I know,' I said to Michael over dinner. 'But there's something about driving down roads which I've seen on films. Like all those streets of San Francisco.'

'Watch it. You're getting the LA bug. You think you know things because you've seen them on film. This city is full of people who live life at one remove.'

'Speaking of which, this restaurant is good, but it is one remove from Mexico. I'm still keen to drive down to Baja, you know. Do you think you'll have the time? To go there like we planned?'

Michael glanced up from his plate. 'I wouldn't say we had a plan. It was just an idea—but an idea I'm working on. It depends how much I get done in the next few days. I have a book for you to read in the meantime.' He passed over a big hardback, richly illustrated: *A History of Mexican Archaeology: The Vanished Civilisations of Middle America*.

Christmas Day. No other day of the year reminded me so strongly of the tensions that drive people apart; of the roads and houses and countries we need to put between ourselves. Now Finn lived in New York, now my whole family was scattered to the four winds, Christmas didn't make sense to me any more. Even if we had all lived in Melbourne I wondered if we'd have managed to defeat the sadness that sprawled out across the suburbs as people tried to gather together the fragments of their families. The pressure to get it right, to get the idea of family right, was intense; no wonder most people buckled under it.

The previous Christmas Eve I had flown in to Hong Kong to meet my dad, who had flown in from Bangkok. The plan was to spend Christmas Day shopping, a present to ourselves for a hard year's work. I'd flown in late at night and the buildings had giant Santas and stars and trees etched out by the lights of the skyscrapers. The cityscape reminded me of *Blade Runner*, a vision of the world that was bleak but compelling. That night I had lain in bed, sweating in the humidity, dreaming vivid dreams of disintegration; of a self that broke down into bands of colour and light, speeding through time and space then reconfiguring in some city of the future. Michael was like that to me, some exciting but ravaged future place, a place where I could become something new.

This Christmas morning Michael and I woke fucking, we must have started in our sleep. I rubbed my face all over him, like a cat, breathed in the smell of him. 'You smell right,' I said.

'So do you.'

'Was that my present?' I asked, after we had had sex.

'No,' said Michael. 'It was mine. Pack your bags for the day, that's my surprise.'

As we were walking out the door, Tony rang. It was Christmas night back home. I let the machine run and listened to Tony wish me the best. He sounded drunk.

'Who's that?' asked Michael.

'No one,' I said. 'Just my housemate.'

We drove west for two hours before we noticed the smoke. Michael wound down the window to let some air into the car and when we opened the window we could smell it.

'There's a fire,' I said.

'We seem to attract these things,' Michael said, peering out the windscreen at the sky.

'Do you know what you're supposed to do if you get caught in one?' I said. 'You curl up in the bottom of the car, cover yourself with wet towels or rugs and let the fire move over you—that's the safest thing. The worst thing to do is get out of the car and try and run away. Fire can move quicker than you.' I looked at him. 'If enough heat was generated the bush would simply explode like a bomb around you.'

'You're very focused,' he smiled wryly, 'when it comes to drama. But I don't think it will come to that.'

We stopped and looked around and could see a glow in the distance. 'That's Joshua Tree,' he sounded irritated. 'Where I was planning on going for our picnic. Now I don't know what to do.'

'Let's keep driving,' I say. 'Take me to Palm Springs. We could stay overnight. We don't have to be back till tomorrow.'

'Stay overnight? I hadn't planned on that.'

'Is it a problem?'

'No,' he hesitated. 'No. I just hadn't planned on it. Look, I think it will be difficult. To find somewhere to stay.'

We spent that night back in Venice. We talked about Mexico, again, but it was dawning on me that we were going nowhere. Michael seemed to have trouble organising himself to do anything at all. He could tell I was becoming annoyed and became solicitous, offering me chocolate biscuits, joints and cups of tea. He lit candles around the room before we went to bed. Despite, or perhaps to distract myself from, my frustration with him, I sucked his cock. It was silky to me. What it did to him, I liked that too. After he came he stroked my head, drew me into his arms. 'You give the best head,' he said. 'I love the way you suck me.' I was irritated all over again. This is not a skill I want to be remembered for. Perhaps Michael could tell he'd said the wrong thing, because he started to play a game we'd played together before, a game in which we tried to remember all the states of America.

'Georgia,' he drawled, in mock Southern accent, 'Alabama, Oregon, Washington, Idaho, Montana, Wyoming, North Dakota, South Dakota,' seeing the map of America before him, 'Minnesota, Wisconsin, Michigan, Iowa, New York, New Jersey, Connecticut, Massachusetts.' He drew breath, 'Thems is only some of the places I've travelled trying to find myself a better head job. I've been to Pennsylvania, Delaware, Maryland, Maine, Vermont, Hawaii, Nebraska, California, Nevada, Utah, Colorado, Arizona, New Mexico, Texas, Kansas, Oklahoma, Arkansas, Missouri, Kentucky, Illinois, Indiana, Ohio, Virginia, West Virginia, Tennessee, South Carolina, North Carolina, Florida…' And before he could say Mississippi, Louisiana, Alaska or the other two states I can never remember the names of, he'd gone hard and I'd gone down on him again.

The next morning we lay in bed late, kissing.

'Why did Roberta leave you?' I asked.

'Where did that come from?' He was holding me close, but his body had gone rigid.

'You told me she met someone else. But why? Why was she looking?'

'What do you mean why? Why does anyone? She was bored of me, I suppose.'

'No, there's something else,' I said. 'Something has happened to you.'

Michael was holding me, stroking my hair. 'Well, actually, there was more to it than that. She kept miscarrying. She would get pregnant and then four weeks or so later she would lose it. Four times it happened. By the last time she was hating me.'

'That is sad,' I said.

'She was right to blame me,' said Michael, 'as it turned out. She got pregnant to what's-his-face within weeks. Happy families.'

He lay on his back, looking blankly at the ceiling. 'You needn't think about her, or worry about that time. It is you,' he paused, awkward. 'It's you I love.'

A day later we were on the way to the airport. Once I knew Mexico wasn't going to happen I decided to go to

New York and spend New Year's Eve with Finn.

'My birthday is on the cusp between Sagittarius and Scorpio,' I say. 'Which star sign should I read?'

Michael took the paper from me and read aloud from it when we next pulled up at the lights: '*Sagittarius, November 22—December 21, for the week December 27 to January 2, 1996. Next week things will have moved on. Something will be over.* That's us.' He chucked the paper over his shoulder onto the back seat. I just sat and stared out the car window, like I had when I was here as a child. Ever since he'd said he loved me he'd been behaving more erratically than ever.

By the time we got to the airport he was tender again. Leant across and held my face.

'Don't look so sad,' I said. 'I'll be back in a few days. You're not saying goodbye forever.'

'It was courageous of you to come and see me after so much time. You're a very brave woman.' He was being formal which I took to mean he was moved. And perhaps he was. But now I can see he was trying to work out how to say goodbye.

Nine

'I want to understand this great love of yours,' says Ruby, 'but frankly, even with all the exotic backdrops, I'm stumped.'

'You have friends who have drug problems,' I say. 'You know about addiction.'

'Is it the same thing?' she asks, and I tell her it is.

'If there is any sense to it, it is this,' I say. 'I loved him *because* he was ambivalent for so many years.'

'You know what Krishnamurti says? *When you get rid of attachment, there will be love*.' Ruby quotes at me. 'He means real love. The opposite of what you're calling love.'

I sigh, trying not to be irritated when Ruby carries on like this, trying not to be defensive because she is looking at me the way all my friends looked at me. I don't blame people for not understanding. I don't understand myself. Ask a heroin user whose addiction has spiralled why that has happened. They can't explain. Ask a drinker—they don't know either. As for me, I could say: 'My fathers left me.' In fact I do say that sometimes, but to be honest it rings hollow; it sounds like bargain-basement Freud. Or 'I was molested,' but that's therapy talk, too. This I am clear about: it is no one else's fault. I *chose,* with a full heart, to give over seven years to the thought of him.

'I can just tell you the facts,' I say. 'I can only tell you what happened.'

We change the subject before things get too fraught. We are eating a meal in Munnar, a tea plantation town. Watery dhal and a curry that is meant to be palak paneer, but the green is wrong and the cheese is off. We have found one piece of chicken in our chicken marsala—the rest is gravy. Despite the promising picture of a bottle of Kingfisher beer on the door, it is an alcohol-free night. When I first travelled in countries where alcohol was hard to come by I simply gave up drinking for the duration of the trip. These days, I don't find that so easy.

'Places change you, don't they?' Ruby says. 'We didn't go there together, but whenever you talk about going to Rajasthan fifteen years ago it sounds like it was just two years ago except that it is more crowded and polluted now. But when I saw the men in turbans and their shoes with curly toes I felt like I had walked into *Arabian Nights*, like you did. I loved it that people painted blue or red or green goats and elephants onto their whitewashed walls. Or if they were Brahmins their entire house was painted blue. There were whole villages of blue houses.'

'It was in Rajasthan that I stood on the roof of my hotel in the fort wall of Jaisalmer,' I say, 'watching tanks move slowly across the desert, throwing up dust, as they drove into Pakistan. That same night I watched a bank of sand roll across the desert towards the fort, forcing its way through the lattice stone work that lined our room. After the storm was over the sand lay on the bedspread in lattice patterns, like the most delicate embroidery.'

'You think you can prepare yourself for somewhere if you have seen pictures, or documentaries or whatever, but nothing is the same as being in a place. Letting it get under your skin.' Ruby pauses. 'I don't think this place will get under my skin, though.'

'Nor mine. I actually thought I'd gone mad this afternoon, when the van dropped us at the Indo-Swiss Cattle Farm.' It was meant to be one of the area's highlights. We admired the calves, were impressed by the size of the bulls and stood, speechless, in front of a patch of garden called the Fodder Crop Museum, which was a series of tufts of different strains of grass labelled in Hindi and English.

'Why is it,' Ruby asks, after we've sat in subdued silence for a while, 'that I want to drink more when it's hot, like now. But I also want to drink more when it's really cold. There is nothing I like more than a swig of brandy after a day in the snow.'

'I find that I like a drink in more moderate temperatures as well.'

We sit thoughtfully for a moment. 'Let's go back to the

room,' Ruby says to me, 'I think there is something to drink there. In the mini bar.' Innocent words, welcome words, but ones I had used with Michael. That time I started a lie with a lie and the echo startles me, all these years later, even though I know Ruby is telling me the truth. Even though she and I aren't playing games.

'Catherine, meet Anna,' said Finn. 'Anna, meet Catherine.'

I was nervous. Finn was my special piece of family, my most loved person in the world and I wasn't sure what I thought about him living here, in New York, with a beautiful American–Italian woman. Anna was smart too. 'I hope you don't mind me saying I'm nervous,' she said, when we met. 'It's just I've heard so much about you.'

New York was a blur of the Calvin Klein ads that papered the boards around building sites in SoHo, or loomed storeys high on the side of buildings mid-town. The city was transforming into one giant billboard. In some ways I was in awe of the sweep of a campaign that bridged years and cities and buildings. Marky Mark had towered over Sunset Boulevard when I first went to Los Angeles, in 1993. On the last day of 1995 it was Kate Moss and heroin chic. The images were black and white, grainy. The city was being swamped by brand names. There were fewer coffee shops that weren't Starbucks, bookshops that weren't Barnes & Noble or Borders. I used to travel to escape what I knew; these days I felt I could find nothing else.

Back then, I had loved this global thing (and even this time I rushed to Baby Gap to buy clothes for Max) but now I saw clearly the erasure of difference; worse, I sensed the closing of escape routes from the sense of claustrophobia that had propelled me away from people and around the world.

Finn thought I was being romantic. 'New York has always been like this,' he said. 'Changing all the time. It's what makes it such a fantastic place to live. This is just a phase.'

'Ah, the scientist speaking. Perpetual motion. But you've got to admit; you have to walk further now to find the grotty streets with the pawnbrokers' and the old gunshops with the fading Winchester signs. You've got bugger all chance of finding clothes shops that aren't Gap or French Connection.'

'When have you ever bought a gun?' Finn laughed. 'These guys aren't just going to stay in business so tourists like you can look at their cute run-down shops.'

'Fuck you.'

'No, I think you mean, fuck *you*.'

'Clothes aren't Finn's strong point,' Anna intervened. 'Don't forget Barney's.'

'You're right,' I said, 'As long as there is Barney's in New York all's right with the world.'

'Tomorrow we'll go on a long walk,' Finn promised. 'We'll go to Brooklyn. Plenty of authentic culture there to cheer you up. Speaking of authenticity, whatever happened to Mexico? I thought you and Michael were going to go down to Baja for a few days.'

'Some work came up for him.'

'For an academic? At Christmas time? That's weird.'

We spent New Year's Day walking down and across to Brooklyn. As we walked along the boardwalk looking back on Manhattan, I had a flash. 'I remember being here,' I said to Finn, 'with Mum. When I was four. You were just a fat baby, you probably don't remember.'

'No, I don't remember that. But I do remember I had a fabulous figure as a baby.'

We wandered around the brownstones and several churches. 'My family used to live around here,' Anna said. 'That was our local church.' She pointed out a tiny stone church with a small white marble angel out the front—so lifelike it seemed as though she might take flight.

'Bondi is more secular,' I tell her, 'we have sculptures of mermaids around my suburb. Or we did, before they rusted.'

'Speaking of where you live,' Finn said, 'and of religion, are you barracking for the Sydney Swans yet?'

'I think this is where I say fuck *you*.'

'You guys,' Anna was getting used to it. 'Though Finn did tell me you changed teams once. Even Americans understand that that is bad behaviour.'

'Do I know you well enough to say, "Fuck you too"?'

'I'd feel honoured,' Anna smirked. 'Like part of the family.'

Finn traipsed behind us while Anna took me to her favourite bookshop, which was full of beautiful art books, and then showed me a vintage clothing store that had been there for twenty years. We'd planned to go for a coffee, but it was so cold we went to a bar and had a whisky instead.

By the time we walked back over the Brooklyn Bridge it was even colder. Our faces hurt where the breeze hit them. I had never seen the city so clear. Manhattan sparkled.

'Could that be clear ice on the buildings that's making them catch the light like that?' I asked. 'Does it get that cold?'

'It does,' Finn said, 'but I've never seen the city looking like this.'

'It's like a city of ice crystals,' Anna says. 'The snow cave out of *The Faerie Queene*.'

The next morning I woke to blizzard warnings on the television. I was in the kitchen making a coffee when Finn wandered in, half asleep. 'You'd better get going early,' he said. 'If you don't get on a plane this morning you'll be snowed in for days and miss LA and all your connecting flights to Australia.' I threw my stuff in my bag. 'I love you,' I said to Finn as I hugged him goodbye.

The snow began to fall as my cab pulled up; by the time I got to the airport there was pandemonium, people everywhere jostling in queues trying to get onto earlier flights. I managed to get one and joined the line at the gate lounge. But as I looked out through the window, out on the snow swirling so thick everything was turning to white, I knew I had missed my chance. Just before we were due to board, the airport called everything to a halt. Neither I nor anyone else was getting any plane anywhere.

'It is not possible to board flight QF 001, flight JAP 900 and flight BA7,' the announcement went. 'It is not possible to return to Manhattan because of the dangerous weather conditions. Please be advised that all airport hotels are full. Due to the nature of the emergency and the numbers of people involved, there will be no food vouchers.'

It was three p.m. and already an eerie dark had fallen. Backpackers started putting tents up in the waiting areas, preparing to sleep it out.

'It'll be okay tomorrow,' said the woman in front of a queue I was standing in for some reason I can no longer recall.

I knew she was wrong, this was going to last for days. The thought of spending a week on an airport floor made me feel like a caged animal, the thought of being away from Michael for any longer seemed even worse.

'What will I do?' I called him in a panic.

'There is nothing you can do,' he said.

'I won't see you tonight,' I said. 'I may not get the chance to see you again.' Trying not to cry.

'There's no need to be melodramatic,' he sounded remote. 'Things will sort themselves out.'

After I had hung up, I went outside into the snow waving a handful of cash at the stranded cabs. The lead driver beckoned me over with a jerk of the head. He didn't much like the idea of being snowed in away from home either, he told me as we gingerly pulled out of the taxi rank—his wife was due to give birth to their first child any day now. And that was all I learned about Robert, apart from his name. Navigating the worsening snowstorm took all his concentration. The windscreen wipers moved slowly, dumping the snowflakes from one side of the windscreen to the other, opening a slowly blinking eyelid through which the road could intermittently and indistinctly be seen. The traffic stretched for miles.

I thought of footage I'd seen of whiteouts in Europe where people had been trapped in their cars for days and frozen to death. I was furious that I'd put myself in such a dangerous situation because of my desperation to get back to Los Angeles—and furiously embarrassed that I'd rung Michael from the airport because I wasn't going to make it back to him. As I sat and fumed, the traffic thinned. My fellow commuters were either home with a stiff drink by now, or they had thrown in the towel and abandoned their cars by the road.

It was five hours before I got back to Manhattan. It was empty, as if a bomb had dropped leaving all the buildings intact. The taxi slid down Third Avenue, literally the only car on the road. With nothing to grip, it was gliding in wild arcs, first to the left, then to the right down the middle of the road. Close to Grand Central Station, Robert gave up.

'Sorry, ma'am, I'm going to have to leave you here,' he said and I found myself standing on the corner of 3rd and 46th, surrounded by suitcases in a bank of snow with flakes falling around me. I started to cry but it was too cold for immobility. I quickly gathered myself together and dragged my bags to a phone box to ring Finn, who told me the trains were still running. He met me at the station in SoHo and helped me drag my bags through the snow to his apartment. I started to cry all over again when we got there and Anna hugged me and put a scotch in my hand.

'I'm sorry you are missing out on LA,' Finn said. 'But it's fun you are staying. Nothing awful about having to spend a few more days with us.'

'It's not that,' I said, 'it's Michael. I only had a couple more days with him and now I mightn't have that.'

'Change your flight back home. Get to Sydney a few days late. It'll be okay.'

'I think I'm just getting spooked,' I said. 'It used to be there was fire when we saw each other. Now it's snow. It's not a good sign. And, to offer a more solid fact, he sounded totally unmoved on the phone when I rang him from the airport.'

Finn rolled his eyes. 'Think laterally: maybe this is a good sign. Perhaps this huge dump of snow represents the depth of your passion for each other. Perhaps it is about smothering the mundane and the day to day with a soft, delicate—yet potentially dangerous—passion.'

'Deep,' I paused. 'Now let's discuss another urgent matter. As we were driving here for five *fucking* hours I was pondering an ethical issue. Have you ever been at a dinner party where you and your friends have discussed whether or not you would eat each other if you were starving to death?'

'Often,' said Finn.

'Never,' said Anna, simultaneously.

'Well I started to ponder this very question earlier tonight when I thought me and Robert were going to be trapped in the snow.'

'So, could you have eaten him?'

'That's the point. I don't think I could've,' I said. 'He was a nice guy. And very skinny.'

'Wimp,' Finn said. 'He would've eaten you in a flash. You've gotta toughen up; this is New York.'

After another scotch I went to bed and slept heavily for a few hours. I woke to find Finn and Anna hanging out the window gazing at the snow that had built up through the night. All the cars were covered and the doorways snowed in. The snow glowed under the street lamps, intensifying what little light there was so it was like a strange twilight, even though sunrise was more than an hour away. More remarkable than the glow was the silence that had enveloped this largest, this noisiest of cities. The snow on the roads had stopped the traffic and muffled all other sounds as well. There was only the occasional echo of voices as the sun rose and people fought their way out into the snow to dig out their cars or bikes and the kids who lived in Finn's apartment block all raced outside to make snowmen.

That morning Manhattan took on a carnival atmosphere. People got out toboggans and snowboards. They went skiing down Fifth Avenue. There was no logic to which shops opened and which didn't. The Swedish lipstick shop opposite Finn's flat was open, but you couldn't get groceries or papers. I went with the flow, and bought several lipsticks—black, dark brown, bright red. When the snowfall had eased enough, we walked around the streets, arms linked.

'When snowflakes bond together they can be as strong as concrete,' Finn told us. 'No two are the same.'

'I know that,' I said, but as we walked along I found myself picking up a handful of snow to examine it, as if I had a chance of seeing an individual flake.

'So admit it,' Finn said. 'You do think I say interesting things.' And, as I began to mould the snow into a snowball to throw at him, I confessed that once in a while I did.

We walked home, through the gentle flurry of snow that was still falling, and I put out my tongue, feeling the prick of cold as the flakes landed. 'If snowflakes are so strong,' I said to Finn, 'how come I can melt them away with my tongue? How come I can disappear them with the heat of my palm?'

'Ah,' Finn said, 'the way to kill a snowflake is to isolate it. Separate it from the pack and pick it off,' before pausing to build up to the bad punchline I could see from a mile off. 'Or perhaps it is just that you have a very strong tongue.'

We hung around the house with the heating up high, reading and ignoring each other. We watched the weather channel. The blizzard had been dubbed The Blizzard of '96 and every snowflake was being reported on a minute-by-minute basis.

'I love it,' I said. 'You would think it was World War Two.'

'This is what you get when there are dozens of cable channels, with one dedicated to weather. This is a content opportunity like they haven't had in years,' said Finn.

Regular bulletins would report the death count. 'I'm not sure,' said Finn, 'that guys in their fifties having heart attacks while trying to clear snow drifts can count as death by blizzard. I'd have thought it should be classified as death by unfitness.'

'And I notice,' continued Anna, 'that there's no talk of the homeless people that must have died under snow or been knifed in overcrowded shelters.'

'Already finishing each other's sentences,' I say. 'That's a good sign.'

Two nights after the blizzard we watched 'Letterman', which, for the first time in its history had almost no studio audience. People watching the show on television saw a window of opportunity and snowboarded through the streets at ten at night, figuring this was their chance to get into the audience. Most of the show was taken up with shots of people running into studio seats and whooping.

Despite the wonderful strangeness of these days I spent far too long in phone queues trying to get a plane ticket out, as if a day or so made a difference. I rang Michael each day and each day he sounded more distant.

'I'm not sure,' I said, 'if I've a ticket out for tomorrow or the day after.'

'Don't stress,' Michael said. 'You'll sort it, I'm sure. But if it takes until the weekend I mightn't be around—I'm thinking of going away with friends.'

'Right,' I said, feeling defeated, not sure what I should expect. Wanting to scream: but aren't you missing me? Do you care? 'Well, I'll let you know.'

'Fine,' he said. 'Ben's over, I'd better go.'

'You two sound very formal with each other,' commented Anna. 'You sounded more relaxed when you talked to your boss and told her you'd miss a couple of days' work.'

'Michael blows hot and cold,' I said. 'Says he's busy or has a friend around so he can't chat. It makes me nervous.'

'I don't have much experience with men,' said Finn.

'In fact I have none. But if he cared about you he wouldn't be doing that. You'd be able to be yourself.'

Finn was right. I realised Michael and I had not been talking as directly to each other in person or on the phone as we had in our emails when we were thousands of miles apart. I found myself on the phone to Marion, pretending to tell her about the blizzard and asking what Max was up to, pretending to be interested in the irony that Melbourne was sweltering with temperatures over thirty degrees while we were sinking deep into snow. But really I was just trying to make sense of things with Michael.

'It's confusing. He was very gentle with me when I first arrived, but something's not quite right. We had lots of great sex…'

'I wondered how long it would be before you got stuck on this,' Marion interrupted.

'Let me finish,' I interrupted back. 'What I was going to say is that after we have the sex it is like my brain stops working. It sounds like I'm making a joke, I know, but it's actually quite extreme. I become really passive, like I'm stoned. I feel unable to be direct. When I was staying there he went out quite a few times and didn't ask me to come along. Every day he said he had to work on some paper or other and was at his desk for hours—even on Christmas night. I felt as if I was in the way—but it's him who asked me here.'

'Sweetheart,' Marion said, 'this stuff is not new. I can't believe we're having this conversation again. He's not good for you. I suspect he's not good for himself. Will you please look after yourself? Please?'

'I will,' I placated. 'I promise.' But after I hung up the phone I realised I didn't really know what this meant: to look after myself. I did not know how to stop the sense that Michael was inside me. Under my skin.

Four days after the blizzard I arrived back in Los Angeles. It was late at night and I caught a cab. I was buoyed up by the drama of the blizzard and the uncomplicated, loving company of my brother and Anna. Michael seemed pleased to see me and smiled broadly as he opened the door. He took my bag then started kissing me hard and quick all over my face, running his hands down my tight leather jacket and nudging me onto the couch. We barely said a word, just smiled and murmured at each other as we removed our clothes.

'What flight are you leaving on?' was the first coherent thing he asked, when we lay in bed the next morning.

'My flight out is in three days,' I said, 'like it would have been if I came back on January 2.'

'Three days? That's difficult,' Michael rolled over. 'I'm not sure that's a good idea.'

I could feel myself shrinking, willed myself not to. 'I told you this on the phone—it's the only flight I could get. A lot of people had to change their travel plans because of all the drama, and fuck you for making me feel so unwelcome.'

'I didn't mean it like that; you're wilfully misinterpreting me. I just meant what I said. That it makes things difficult.' He got up, angry, walked into the bathroom and shut the door.

'In what way?' I opened the door, stood there, belligerent.

'Work,' he said. 'I've got a lot on.'

I left the house and spent that day walking around Venice. Hidden in the back streets were spectacular modern houses in amongst the old: metallic boxes next to Spanish villas next to run-down weatherboard cottages. It was full of palm trees and spiky jagged gardens. Claes Oldenburg binoculars standing three-storeys high, Frank Gehry bars and houses. By the next day I was bored and restless in the way that you can only be when you are waiting for someone else to make things okay. Michael worked and I shopped. I bought things that caught my eye: a pretty dress, some CDs, a bright red Mexican crucifix with soft-drink tops nailed into it. When I went to put my purchases away I found the things I had left behind when I went to New York in a plastic bag at the bottom of the cupboard. I noticed for the first time that the candles he had around the room, that he had lit when I was first here, were much lower than when they'd last been lit for me.

The next day, my last day, Michael went out for a few hours. 'I've kept this afternoon free,' he said. 'For you.'

I sat around and waited, reading. Michael came home

for lunch, as he had promised. As he was serving the gnocchi he had brought with him, I took a photo.

'Stop it,' he said, as I went to take the shot. 'You know I hate having my photo taken.' I still have the picture: the scowl on his face, his body twisting away from me, his hand held up towards his face as he tried to cover it.

'What is it with you and cameras?' I asked, flustered. Michael shrugged, irritated. 'I don't want to argue,' he said. 'Let's go and look at those second-hand bookshops I told you about. I've been meaning to do that since you arrived.'

We wandered down Main Street, holding hands, then turned into a small side street where there was a ramshackle bookshop that was a cafe as well. People sat around in old armchairs and read. Michael and I spent a couple of hours looking around.

'Look at this,' said Michael, at one point. 'For a moment I thought it was a first edition of the English translation of *Les Liaisons Dangereuses*. That would be worth more than $2000. But alas, it's only a tenth edition.'

'I bought a less fancy but still very gorgeous edition of that book for you two years ago,' I said. 'Then didn't give it to you because you were four hours late for dinner one night.'

'Don't start,' he said. 'We're trying to have a nice time here.'

I had a flash to the scene in the film I had hated but had not been able, after all these years, to get out of my head. Malkovich stiffly rejecting Michelle Pfeiffer, repeating over and over, 'It is totally beyond my control.' Then remembered what Michael had said to me that first time we argued, that one day I'd understand, and I thought about what Marion had said about giving bad behaviour more dignity than it deserved by dressing it up as romance and literature. Sometimes I felt as if I had half a dozen conversations running around in my head, from the past, and from imagined futures. With people and books and films. It was exhausting.

'Catherine?' Michael said again, but this time putting an arm around my shoulder and giving me a squeeze. 'You've vagued out on me. Let's go. We'd better get home if we want to be out again this evening. Look, I bought you a book.' He was smiling at me. Cheered up, perhaps, by my disengagement.

'The *Lonely Planet Guide to Mexico*?'

'It's only six months old,' he said, looking pleased with himself.

'But we're not going there,' I said. 'It will be well out of date before I ever get there.'

'You'll just have to come back soon, then, won't you?' He kissed me on the cheek. 'Let's go.'

That night we went to a Japanese bar in the hills above Hollywood and sat looking down over Los Angeles. The pollution lent intensity to the sunset; the sun was a ball of dark red, the sky and haze around it deep orange.

'Why is it that pollution makes things so beautiful?' I asked.

'If you want to see unnatural beauty, wait till it gets darker and watch the planes taking off and landing at LAX.'

Michael was right. As the sun went down the lights on the planes became brighter and it was like watching dozens of shooting stars fly west over the sea, east over the city. We sat together quietly for a while. Watching them.

'Why is it,' Michael asked, abruptly, 'that you haven't got a boyfriend? Someone like you? I don't understand.'

'I don't know,' I said. Not telling him the truth: that there was Tony, but I had never met anyone I'd wanted as much as Michael.

'You understand that this can't last, don't you?' said Michael. 'Not once you leave here.'

'No I don't understand,' I said. 'Why can't it?'

'How could it? I've done the distance thing before. I'm not doing it again. We just can't do it.'

'We can,' I was surprised at my forcefulness. 'In fact, we have been, in a fashion, for almost three years now. You are making things more difficult than they need to be. You say you will be coming out at Easter. I'll be back again for work in June. If things keep going on and we make it to the end of the year I'd be prepared to move here. To be with you.'

Michael looked flustered, looked at the barman. 'Two more margaritas,' he said. Then, after a few minutes, said quietly, 'It's not that I don't want to, it's that I don't trust myself,' he said. 'I just don't think that I can do it.'

'But we could try,' I was insisting. I had never wanted anything so much. The more he resisted me the more certain I felt.

'I just don't think that I can do it,' he said again.

I woke up that final morning at dawn, hungover, knowing I had to pack and leave. The alcohol had made me all jangly and nervous. In the face of the damage I was doing to myself over Michael I simply dropped all my defences, and my main memory of that morning is of the most intense vulnerability. I arrived, briefly, at the moment I always pursued with Michael. The moment when we both moved as one, when I was outside myself, when I glimpsed what I called spirit. And the thing about Michael is that for all that things were wrong between us, we could do this for each other. There were seconds when we could be in each other's company and be truly, intensely happy. I could feel that he loved me, my skin vibrated with the knowledge; it was on his lips, in his fingertips. He felt my belly, stroked my breasts. 'You're full,' he said. 'You're silk. You're...beautiful.' It was true that my body had swollen over the time I was with him, at the thought of him, under his touch.

We made love slowly and for hours. I would think minutes had passed and glance at the clock by the bed to see that more than an hour had gone by. I curled into a ball, he fucked me from behind, his fingernails gently scratching the small of my back. I was like an animal, mewing, breathing heavily. I couldn't speak. Michael, usually voluble during sex, finally was at a loss for words.

Ten

'I want us to go to Land's End at the tip of India,' Ruby says. 'I think you'll like it there.'

'I'm sure I will,' I say, 'but it's ten hours in a bus in the opposite direction from where we planned to go next.'

'It's a sacred place,' she says, firmly. 'You are here to rediscover your spirituality, and I've organised us a lift.'

We're driven there by a middle-aged Indian couple Ruby met when she was watching the cricket on TV at our hotel in Munnar.

'We are here in the tea plantations for our second honeymoon,' Gita told Ruby. 'Now our children have all left home.' Gita and her husband, Rajeev, both grew up in Uganda but they met in Bombay after they'd been forced out by Amin during the seventies. Now they live in London.

'Our marriage was arranged,' Gita tells us on the drive. 'So it was not like falling madly in love. Actually I loved someone else.' Rajeev drives on stoically. 'My first boyfriend, he was better looking than Rajeev. But not as rich and not from such a good family.'

I start to laugh, then stop myself, for fear of offending them. I needn't worry. They have told this story many times before.

'I had a very sexy girlfriend myself,' Rajeev says. 'More sexy than Gita, but also, not as rich.' Gita starts to laugh, then Rajeev joins in. They crack each other up.

'Actually,' Gita recovers herself. 'Our love was slow to come, but now it is good. Sometimes we are quite bored, but mainly, we love each other very much.'

Rajeev turns around and winks at Ruby who is in the back seat. 'When it is too boring,' he says, 'I can always watch the cricket.'

'This is a very nice hotel,' Gita says when they drop us off. 'Rajeev, why aren't we staying at this hotel?'

It is a very nice hotel. I am taken aback. 'I booked it,' Ruby says. 'Special for us. Let's dump our stuff. It is not far off sunset and I want to give you a present.'

I don't understand the connection between these two things, but we walk down through the fishing village, and the shell shops for tourists and pilgrims. Ruby leads me through the tangle of touts to a patch of ocean that has rocks banked up all around, creating an artificial lagoon. The water is full of women in saris and men in dhotis. They squeal and flick water at each other before reluctantly going under.

'Come,' Ruby says. 'Follow me.'

She walks to the water line and then keeps on going, full-length skirt, long-sleeved shirt and all. She turns to make sure I'm behind her.

I join her at about waist height and then we hold our noses and go under together, trying to ignore the colour of the water. It is putrid and brown.

After we have done that she hugs me then puts a hand on my shoulder, and holds me at arm's length. She says to me, formally, 'This is where the Indian Ocean, the Bay of Bengal and the Arabian Sea meet. Gandhi's ashes were spread here, where we are standing. That is why it is a sacred place. That is why you must wash yourself here. It is something like the Christian notion of washing away your sins—it leaves you open for life's blessings. Like you said when we first met, this is an important time for you: you are being reborn in all directions.' She kisses me cere-moniously on the forehead.

It is a nutty, lovely thing to do. I smile at her, kiss her back.

'As an added bonus, this is one of the few places in the world where you can see the sunset and the moonrise at the very same moment—every April. Since it's September we will have to make do with watching the sun set tonight, and being able to see the sunrise tomorrow, while standing at practically the same point.'

'I love this kind of cosmic symbolic stuff, you know that, don't you?'

'Of course I know,' Ruby says, looking proud of herself. 'Do you think I'd have gone to all this trouble if I didn't?'

Later that night I am woken by a thunderstorm that doesn't quite come. The sky is rumbling and there are bolts of lightning, but no rain. It is like the song from *Lagaan* says, *Let loose not the sword of lightning, but the arrows of raindrops!* I sit up and shake myself, hoping that if I can properly wake, perhaps I might properly rest. I look across at Ruby. Her face is angled towards a shaft of moonlight that has broken through a gap in the clouds. I sit, wakeful, and watch her sleep.

Tony was waiting for me at Sydney airport, which surprised me but made me happy. We had exchanged the occasional email while I was away, and it seemed to me from the emails, from the fact he was here, that he wanted to forget our fight so we could go back to being friends. I launched into the details of my trip but I hadn't judged things between us right. He cut across me. 'Enough,' he said. 'It's the blizzard I want to hear about, not Michael. I get the picture. Full moon and fire gone. Waning moon and snow instead. You are such a hippy. But in this case, go with the signs. I think they're right. He's a jerk; I don't know what you see in him. He's not even good looking, like me.'

'His nose isn't as big though,' I said, pushing my luck even further in an attempt to get us back to how things had been. To my immense relief, he laughed.

'Take me to the beach,' I drew him into a hug. 'I want to swim. I have been pining for Bondi.'

When we got to the water and I dived into the waves, I finally felt I had come home. It was cold and refreshing and to be so close to the sea, to spend the day in and beside it, felt like a blessing. In the afternoon we went together on one of my favourite walks on the North Shore, around from the Taronga Zoo to Clifton Gardens, where the bush was so thick that, if it wasn't for the sight of the occasional ferry heading past on its way to Manly, you would think you were in the middle of the country. To add to the adventure spiders' webs, in the middle of which sat big fat spiders, were strung from one side of the path to the other—sometimes a dozen in only a hundred metres.

Tony had packed a picnic for us and after walking for an hour or so we sat on the lawn that led down to the beach at Clifton Gardens and ate crusty bread with avocado.

'Do you think I should listen to him when he says he loves me, or when he says it's over?' I couldn't help myself.

'You really must be losing it if you think it is okay to talk to me about this shit. After what happened between us.'

I went to speak, but then didn't, because he was right. This thing—and it was more than Michael, I knew that—was bigger than me and it left me with no judgment.

'I'm going to let you off the hook this time,' Tony went on, 'because I drove all my friends crazy when I was breaking up with Julia.' He put his hand over mine. 'I don't approve, and I need you to shut up. But I understand.'

Michael didn't answer my emails, calls or letters in the weeks after I returned. Tony made it clear he was still interested in sleeping with me, in more than that, but I was too confused to take him up on it. Instead, we lived like an old married couple. We cooked and shopped together, went to the movies, and cuddled on the couch in front of bad TV.

One night we went to see *Portrait of a Lady*. I had loved the book and felt trepidation about both the film and another couple of hours in front of John Malkovich. I groaned when I realised one of the ads I had helped design was going to run in the trailers. A group of happy-go-lucky young people, barefoot, casually dressed, sit down to a pile of oysters on a boat that could be in Haloong Bay, or Lakes Entrance or the Blue Grotto. The vibe is comic, they are gorging themselves on food and drink. As they collapse, one by one, on comes the voiceover: *At Freedom, the world is your oyster.*

The audience guffawed and there were a couple of boos. A bad joke, I thought, but it's got their attention. I leant over to Tony. 'If they don't like that, wait till they see the next one—"We leave no stone unturned."'

He laughed. 'I do think you may be getting bored.'

'I know. The tragedy is it's the most successful ad campaign we've done. The less I try, the better things seem to go.'

It was clear that Marion and Tony had been discussing me behind my back. 'How can you turn down Tony, who is there, for Michael who isn't?' she said to me on the phone one night. 'That's totally aside from whether Michael behaves himself when he is actually in the same place as you.'

'It depresses me to admit this,' I replied, 'but I sometimes think that it is because he is far away that I love him.' I paused. 'I try, but I never get that intense about people who are close to me. Friends who support me. People like you.'

'You'll lose Tony,' she said, 'if you haven't already. Will that worry you?'

'I've no idea,' I said. 'I'm in this constant state of grief, and I call it Michael. But perhaps if Tony gives up on me I will call the grief Tony. Who knows.'

'I'd call it Dad if I were you. Have you thought of seeing a shrink?'

I admitted that was a good idea but I never followed up on the name she gave me, or the one Tony gave me a couple of weeks later.

'You're sick,' Tony said after he came home to find me watching some crap show for the fourth night that week. 'Too much of your emotional life is vicarious or mediated by technology. Computers. Video. Pretend stuff. Let me put this as bluntly as I can: George Clooney is not your boyfriend. You do not work in an emergency ward in a Chicago hospital. A girl like you should be aiming for a real boyfriend.'

'I'm used to relationships being in my head. And, given the hours I'm working, it's useful I think like that.'

'It's true,' said Tony. 'Relationships '90s style. Very cost-efficient. In the short term at least.'

'Do you think it's a government plot?' I laughed. 'To bring up a generation so hooked on the fantasy of perfection and endless possibility that we never have the kind of family life that may cut down on productivity? Perhaps it was something they put in the water along with fluoride. And I have to tell you, I have fantastic teeth. No fillings.'

'We didn't have fluoride where I grew up,' Tony smiled toothily at me, 'yet I also have fantastic teeth. I think this may be another of your dubious theories.'

I'd go down to the beach early every morning and launch myself, swimming further and further each day. For the first couple of weeks I could only make it one way across Bondi, could only get as far as the point where the floor of the ocean moved towards me. Soon after that rocks began, then the seaweed and fish darting in amongst them. Then, one very calm day, I got to the point where I could stand on the rocks beside the wall of the Icebergs pool. Soon I was turning at Icebergs and heading back north again. Some days I felt so strong I could imagine I was swimming across the oceans of the world: the Indian Ocean, the Atlantic Ocean, the Caribbean Sea.

Some days the waves were so high I couldn't see over them. I'd become disorientated and find I was swimming out to sea. While it was more dangerous swimming when the surf was up, it was more exciting as well. The water swelled underneath me and if the waves were particularly high they would drop me quickly back to sea level and there would be a flash of fear, followed by delight.

The repetition of strokes and the endless ripples on the sand below me would lull me as if I were meditating. I was no longer attached to the land, or the city. I was carried by the water, as well as moving through it like the fish I passed, the seaweed trails that traced the movement of currents.

If I didn't swim I'd walk, as the sun was rising, around the cliffs to Bronte past the Icebergs pool where men had been swimming, literally, among iceblocks every winter since 1929. Walking this path, day after day, I began to relish its particular curves and quirks. The sea was sometimes calm and green, other times rough and grey. Some wild mornings I'd be caught out as the rain came down in sheets and I'd remember people talking about Black Sunday, February 6, 1938, a day when the weather turned and the surf became so huge that three hundred people had to be rescued and five people drowned.

Even if there was no rain I often came home wet from the foam and spray where the waves curled up the cliff back onto the path, heavy as a shower. At the point, the wind always hit with a force so great I could feel the full weight of the weather slapping my face and skin; I could literally lean out against it.

One day, when I was catching the train home in the evening, I saw an accident. There were some renovations being done at Central Station and metal dividers were placed at awkward angles everywhere, funnelling the peak hour push-and-shove in closer together than usual. As I was going up the escalators I looked down to the platform over the surging mass of people to see that an old man had caught his leg in the divider and fallen. He was lying at such a sharp angle I could only assume the leg was broken, but people were walking around him and someone even walked over him. He was a tough old bastard though; as I watched he reached out and grabbed a woman by the ankle. She stopped and looked at him.

'You,' he commanded. 'Help me. I've broken my leg.'

I told Tony about it that night. 'It was living proof of those surveys. The greater the numbers of people around the less likely people are to help each other. Everyone hopes someone else will sort out the problem. No one takes responsibility.'

'Cities,' Tony looked sad, 'can be horrible places. Much as I love Sydney, I miss Melbourne. It's smaller, things like that don't happen as much. Did the woman help him?'

'She did. She cleared the crowd away from him, called over some guards. But I don't think she would have stopped if he hadn't reached out for her.'

That night Tony and I drank wine and ate together. He flirted with me and did his best to dispel my bad feelings about Sydney. Yet still I went to bed wondering why it was I had moved from Melbourne, where people would look out for me. I pined for Marion and Raff, phoning them almost daily. We talked about Max, and tried to hold on to the inconsequential chat that bound us together.

The pull between the physicality of Sydney and the love of my friends confused me, just as Melbourne confused me. I didn't know what to think of it. It was flat, it housed the people I loved, it made me claustrophobic. Other places…other places were where my family was from. Other places were where I found lovers. But there was something else as well. Like Michael, I needed distance to love people.

'Darling,' Tony said, ' I have something to tell you.'

It was a hot day and we were lying on the sand, drying off from a swim. Tony was scratching his thigh with his left hand, the pressure making his right hand twitch, like when a dog scratches itself. He was like a dog when he came out of the water too, when he shook his curls dry.

'I think I should call you Fido,' I said, not listening to what he was saying.

'I had sex last night,' he announced with a smug look. I felt as if I had been slapped. I must have looked like it, too.

'I didn't mean to upset you,' he reached out and touched my face. 'I didn't think you would care. After all, I'm not Phantom Man, he of the large penis and super brain.'

I burst into tears. 'Stop it,' I said. 'I always hoped that when we were ready, one way or another, we might get together again.'

Tony kissed me on the forehead. 'When are you going to be ready for that? I'll be an old man.'

'You are being cruel,' I said. 'You don't need to rub salt into the wound.'

'I want to,' said Tony. He was angry now. 'I want you to see how bad it is. What you are doing to yourself.' My being upset, my revealing, too late, that I cared, had pissed him off completely. 'Did you think I was going to keep finding you attractive the way you've been moping around, watching crap television and being miserable?'

'I thought you liked crap television.' I was hurt.

'I was pretending,' he said.

'Fuck you. I've got the message.'

'No you haven't, that is what I'm trying to tell you. You

haven't got the message at all.' He got up, shook himself free of sand, of me, and walked towards the ramp, away from the beach.

Tony was hardly home after that. Was it the loss of Tony or was it the months without any contact from Michael? Whatever the reason I was like a cat on a hot tin roof. I read magazines because I couldn't concentrate long enough to read books. Everything seemed magnified, tick tick tick every second of the clock, the phone too loud, the phone didn't ring enough. I would check the email once, five times, ten times a day. I would check the mailbox; I would check my messagebank at home and at work. I carried a mobile phone. Just in case. If I missed a call it could ruin everything. I might miss out on sex, I might miss out on love and marriage and a family. I was surfing adrenalin, underneath the waters were deep. Give way and I would sink into them. So I stayed up, skimming. Coffee, alcohol, dope, food. Stuff. I had to get stuff into me.

Friends asked me why I was like this and I sympathised. I didn't understand either. Yes, Michael was smart, and charming, he was enticingly erratic, alluring, out of reach. But basically this thing, it didn't make sense. I can only come back to this: the sex was extraordinary.

There was this too. Things in my body, in my brain didn't feel right. It was not just other people who thought I was mad, I was starting to feel mad myself. I was starting to understand that other people didn't feel anxious all the time. I knew that the rationality of scientific explanation would never do justice to my, or anyone's, experience of longing, but I began to give up my insistence that what was happening was particular to me. To call what happened chemical was less poetic than calling it love, but it was starting to feel closer to the truth. I'd always called my attraction to Michael chemical, talked about it as if he was a part of my body—so perhaps I might expel him, like a toxin, out of my system.

'Hi, you've called Michael O'Maera. I'll be in Sydney until mid-July, but leave a message, I'll be checking in.'

'*Fuck*,' I screamed, startling people around me. 'You are un-*fucking*-believable.' I slammed down the phone, banged my head against the side of the booth. I was standing at LAX, breaking the promises I had made to Marion and Tony not to call Michael when I got here. But they had had nothing to worry about: we'd passed in the air. He had booked a ticket to fly to Sydney the day I left. *The past is another country,* I was thinking, *they do things differently there*—that was the line that kept coming into my head. HSC English Lit.; *The Go-between*. But what the hell that was trying to tell me I didn't know, or why all I could think about was a line from a book I had studied more than fifteen years before. *Reader, I married him*, was another one of my favourite lines and that wasn't making much sense either. I'm one of the best-read people I know but it was clear from the fact that I was standing in an airport concussing myself in a phone booth that it had done me no good. No fucking good at all.

Sitting on the plane on my way to Chicago I watched *Groundhog Day* for the fifth time. Watched Bill Murray try and figure out how to get things exactly right with the appalling Andie McDowell. Leaving ice-cream on the window ledge, which flavour did she like, should he speak French, should he quote poetry, should they have a snow-ball fight and how hard should he throw the snowball, how many days and months of days and years of days would he try and figure out how to get things right before he stopped trying and got on with the endless day that was his life.

I couldn't watch the film any more. I pulled out a book Tony had given me ('Some light reading for your big fat hippy streak'). It was called *The Tibetan Book of Living and Dying* and it looked like up-market self help. I had read all those. *Women Who Love Too Much*. *Men Who Can't Love*. All that stuff which promised women if they just fixed themselves up everything would be different. But in the book Tony gave me I read a poem that made sense of things.

> *I walk down the street. / There is a deep hole in the side-walk. / I fall in. / I am lost...I am hopeless / It isn't my fault. / It takes me forever to find a way out.*

> *I walk down the same street. / There is a deep hole in the sidewalk. / I pretend I don't see it. / I fall in again. / I can't*

believe I'm in the same place. / But it isn't my fault. / It still takes me a long time to get out.

I walk down the same street. / There is a deep hole in the sidewalk / I see it is there. / I still fall in…it's a habit/ My eyes are open / I know where I am / It is my fault. / I get out immediately.

I walk down the same street. / There is a deep hole in the sidewalk / I walk around it.

I walk down another street.

When I got to Chicago I sent Tony an email: 'Hello my friend,' I wrote. 'I've begun reading the book you gave me. I think, I hope, I am at stage #3.'

I dragged myself around Chicago where there was an international travel conference. I spent my days in an exhibition centre that was like one long shopping mall. There was no light, no air, just a tomb a mile long with four thousand travel agents. As well as the stalls there was a series of morning focus groups where different travel agents 'shared' their global strategies. Buying entire islands seemed a particularly popular 'strategy'.

'More control,' the head of Global Adventures beamed. 'More flexibility to meet our clients' needs.'

Freedom organised some seminars of its own for an hour at the end of each day where the company discussed 'strategies for the new millennium'. There was a lot of talk of branding and the suggestion that the company move into travel guides to compete with the *Lonely Planet*-style guides. The manager of our Los Angeles office had ideas for a line of travel products: backpacks, little clothes lines, inflatable pillows, foil blankets for those who find themselves stuck in the Himalayas somewhere without shelter. Then there was a long angry session about ethics, and the company's responsibility towards the groups they subcontracted out to.

'It is not our problem that the trekking companies we deal with don't pay their porters properly,' said Justin, who ran the London office. 'We've all heard stories about people who have given the porters down coats or good boots, only to see them for sale in the markets after they finish the trek. They choose to live this way.'

'That's bullshit,' I said. 'Poverty is never a "lifestyle" decision, but that's what you make it sound like.'

Tom, from the Dublin office, joined in. 'If we are to continue any pretence that we are an alternative company, we have to take the ethics of the people we subcontract to seriously.'

Trish, the owner of Freedom Travel, began to look animated. 'You're right, Tom. We are an ethical company. Frankly it is one of our assets, something we should be advertising.'

I knew my days in advertising were almost over. I was selling choice and I didn't believe it existed. The global melding imagery in my early ads, the questionable humour of my later ones, those days were over. Smallness and difference were back in, precisely because they were endangered. Being ethical was part of our branding and the idea of making sexy what we should all have been doing without hesitation made me feel sick.

'Fuck the new millennium,' I said to Tom over a beer in his hotel room later that night. 'Fuck Freedom Travel.'

'What kind of hard-hitting Aussie businesswoman are you, in your cups after only two beers? I thought you sheilas were big drinkers.'

I smiled at him. 'I'm a hopeless drinker. Always have been. While we're on the subject, what kind of Irishman are you, drinking lemonade?'

'I'm a drunk,' he smiled. 'So I don't.'

I hadn't really given him a second glance before he'd got into the debate this afternoon, but now I was taking more notice—the brown eyes, the curly hair, the wicked accent.

'Why is it,' I went on, 'that the more I have fetishised choice—sold it, packaged it, lived it—the less I've actually had?'

'How much did you have to start with, I wonder? We're all stuck with our own psyche, not to mention our national psyche. Most choice is marketing, always has been. Take Ireland. Five hundred years as a run-down joke; now we're sexy. None of it makes much difference though a few of us get richer from it. The coffee's got better, the

Guinness has got worse. UK publishers make a shit-load out of a few Irish writers, but an Irish language writer is lucky to get published anywhere at all. Even if you do have a lot of choice, choice for its own sake is pretty meaningless. It's depressing.' He paused. 'What'll you do when the conference is over?'

'Drive,' I said. 'I've got a ticket to Seattle to worship at the shrine of Kurt Cobain—don't laugh—and from there I want to drive to LA. I want to do my own personal road trip, and heal a broken heart with wide open spaces.'

'What's happened to your heart?' he asked and I told him, in as few words as possible.

'How long did you say this has been going on?' he asked.

'Five years,' I said, blushing, putting my head in my hands. 'Shoot me, someone.'

'In AA we have a saying along the lines of "to keep doing the same thing and expect a different result is madness".'

'I know,' I said. 'Believe me. That's why I'm doing the long drive.'

'I'm going to play you Joni Mitchell,' he replied. 'A track for a girl who is heading off on a long drive through California while she's stuck on someone.'

Oh will you take me as I am / Strung out on another man / California I'm coming home.

*

191

As I prepared for my long drive I thought of some of the others I'd done. Of the car trips that had imprinted themselves on me. I remembered that when my mum got with my dad, we spent our Christmases along the wild coast between Apollo Bay and Portland. I could remember the first time I went there, when Finn and I were still little.

I realise now that I was with Mum and Dad on their first real holiday together and my memory of that time is infused with the love that was growing between them. Not every child is lucky enough to see her parents fall in love. I saw them fall out of love as well, and when I was a teenager things ended for them. Now I'm an adult I have trouble remembering the details of that sad time, but I can remember these, the good times, as if they were yesterday.

We had no tents; we slept under the sky, or packed like sardines into the back of the Holden station wagon if it rained. My dad dived for abalone and we would grill it on the fire. I always thought it was tough and refused to eat it. Nowadays it is considered a rare delicacy.

In this part of my memory it is always summer and there are endless days of playing in the sand, of swimming and the smell of campfires and mosquito coils. There were bad things, too, but not very bad, more the kind of things that make something more exciting to remember. There was the time my dad swallowed a bull-ant that was in his beer and he got bitten inside his throat and it swelled up. There was the possibility of snakes—every fallen branch a possible culprit to be inspected from afar. The excitement when one of these sticks uncoiled in a powerful wave across the path and my dad had to kill it with an axe.

I learnt to snorkel in a rock pool and I learnt to dogpaddle. Even today whenever I duck dive, then come to the surface blowing water out of the snorkel in a spout, I have a rush of memory for Dad and the rock pool he taught me to swim in.

I was highly attuned to the love between my parents and hyper-vigilant for signs that it might not work out. I would roll into a ball and face the wall whenever I heard raised whispers, my parents' failed attempt to hide the fact they were fighting. I would close my eyes and think of things that were like dreams, except I was awake. As a child I called them almost-dreams. I would almost-dream of beaches and playing in the sand. Of planes and a train that travelled for days. Of a city that was all stone and bricks and rows upon rows of brownstones. Sometimes these imaginings would roll seamlessly into real dreams, other times they would not stop the rage of the adults in the next room from leaking under the door to find me in my bed.

Over time my imaginings of other places turned into something else. Instead of travel and movement it was thoughts of boys and the new feelings in my body that took me out of myself, away from the world, into sleep. I would dream that a boy and I were forced together by circumstance. Perhaps we would be kidnapped and locked in a barn together and, after a few weeks of forced proximity, he would come to see my true beauty and ravish me.

Perhaps we would be thrown into the back of a truck together, hands tied, and find a way to make love despite being bound. I can remember my first orgasm. The intensity of it. The purity of the pleasure.

As I got older, as I involved other people in my sexual explorations, as I became more consciously sexual, the pleasure lessened. I had to chase harder to find the feelings. What began as an opening to pleasure became a way of closing down. Sex became like the dreams of travel, something so sweet, so powerful, that I forgot the point of them. Both took me out of myself until it seemed there was no getting back.

Eleven

'Is that Princess Di?' Ruby asks, and I realise that it is, that there are dozens of paintings of her on the houses lining the main road of the village we are passing through. Her blonde fringe hangs low, she looks out from underneath it with bright blue eyes. Some portraits are well executed, some more like cartoons. The whole village is a shrine to her.

We are driving to another shrine, the Sthanumalay-aswami Temple. From the outside this temple looks like any other. Square and tiered with row upon row of brightly coloured gods reaching up towards the heavens. Ruby and I take our shoes off and walk gingerly through the mud, past the doors, which are two storeys high and are each made from a single piece of wood.

It is like stepping through the wardrobe door into Narnia, another world. Priests are everywhere, three white stripes painted across their forehead. They wear white dhotis around their waists, their chests are bare, their bodies shiny with coconut oil. There is hardly any natural light here, just the flickering dark yellow light of ghee lamps. The air is thick with oil, with the smells of ghee and of coconut.

There is a monotonal chant in a woman's voice humming over loudspeakers. It is the first woman's voice I have heard in any Hindu temple. To my right is a giant Nandi, the Bull that Siva rides, and Hanuman—a man with a monkey head—some three metres high. The stone on these statues is black, rubbed with oil by worshippers who have been coming for twelve hundred years. To my left is a boulder more than eighteen hundred years old with epigraphs written on it in ancient Pali.

One of the priests takes us in hand. He points to each of the stripes on his forehead. 'Brahma the Creator, Vishnu the Preserver,' he says. 'Siva the Destroyer.' He takes us to a large open chamber with stone columns, floor to ceiling. The columns are organic in shape, more like groups of three or four narrow pipes clustered together. He walks towards one set of pipes, beckoning us to follow. He cups the side of my head and forces my ear to it, then does the same to Ruby. He raps his knuckles on the pipe. The sound is pure.

'A perfect G,' says Ruby.

He raps a different pipe.

'That was a B-flat.'

'Stone,' the priest says. 'All stone.'

He takes us next to a tiny Ganesa chamber that is too small to enter. All we can do is dip our heads low, look in. There are yellow and orange markings painted on him, he is covered in flowers. I bow to him, one of India's favourite gods, the Remover of Obstacles. This Ganesa, like all Ganesas, has only one tusk and he holds his second tusk before him as a stylus.

Our priest takes us to another chamber, but instead of coming in with us, gestures for us to go in alone. It is like stepping into a black hole, it seems entirely lightless in this room. After a few moments, after my eyes adjust, I can make out rows of Kalis, multi-armed, at head height.

'Kali is the consort of Siva,' Ruby says. 'Kali is time.' Then she quotes, *'In the power of Time all colours dissolve into darkness. All shapes return to shapelessness in the all-pervading darkness of the eternal light.'*

In front of me is a stone column with a bowl carved into it, but no lingam.

'Is that a Yoni?' I ask.

'Yes,' Ruby says. 'In theory Hindus believe that there is only divinity when opposites co-exist. Male *and* female. But most of the time you just see the lingam. This is a special place.'

It is hard to describe what it feels like: the energy here is dark and wild, not just in this chamber but throughout the whole temple. When we step out the priest taps our foreheads, then taps the door of the chamber. 'Woman,' he says. 'Very important.'

We go further into the centre of the temple. The ceilings are so low we cannot stand up straight. The air feels heavy in here, as if we are underground. The light is a dim flickering the colour of old gold. The chanting is loud, a combination of the woman's voice over the speakers and the murmurings of the people queueing to go into the central chamber. Eyes full of smoke, ears full of sound. Shirtless men prostrate themselves at the chamber entrance, placing first their forehead, then each cheek onto the cool of the stone floor. They do it over and over.

We bend down to look in and I see many doors, each leading to smaller and darker rooms. It is like looking into a diminishing corridor, perspective seems distorted. I do not know what is in the final room, though this place vibrates with the dangerous power of Siva, and I wonder if it is him in there. There is the merest suggestion of light, one flickering ghee lamp.

It is hard to breathe. My heart is racing, and from the way Ruby is standing, with her hand over her left breast, I can tell hers is as well. There is only one way I can describe what I am feeling: we are looking at time. It tumbles back in this space, not just hundreds, but thousands of years. Backwards through those turbulent centuries when Mohammed, then Christ, then Buddha were born, to the time of the gods and goddesses that came before them.

I don't want to leave but the priest tugs our arms. 'Sivalingham,' he says gesturing back to the chamber we have been looking at, before taking us back to the light of day, to a corridor of columns. As he walks past one he taps it and when Ruby and I go to look at it we see carved into the stone a man sucking his own penis, the shaft standing the full length of his body. The priest walks slowly past the columns, tapping them to draw our attention to a series of such carvings: a woman copulating with a dog, another with a snake, men and women bent over each other in stylised poses.

We are back at the entrance and the priest nods that it is over. We give him money and then we are outside again, feeling slightly shell-shocked. More shocked again when we see a pilgrim standing in front of us, face painted, stripes on his chest, hair in dreadlocks, a spear piercing his tongue and two pieces of metal through his eyebrows. He holds his begging bowl before him but doesn't register our presence, or the coins we place in the bowl. His devotion, his trance, are absolute.

We sit in the car going back to Kanniyakumari in silence. It is some minutes before Ruby says, finally. 'Hinduism is right. Sex and spirituality…they are, well they should be, the same thing.'

'Sometimes,' I say, 'we take just the one thing, sex, and put it in the place of spirit. I did that. That's why the whole Michael thing was so pathetic: it was just a case of bad wiring. If I'd started taking the anti-depressants earlier it never would have gone on so long.'

'Looking for spirit in a relationship doesn't mean you

need drugs,' Ruby says. 'I like that you looked for such things in sex, even if it was with the wrong person. Drugs like that are never an answer.'

'You don't know that. If you figure out where the light at the end of the tunnel is you can use them to get you there. Through the darkness.'

Her disapproval about such things, about the lifeline I found for myself, hurts me. But it's her ignorance that's making me angry. I turn and look out the window at India, waiting for the surge of fury to subside. I stare out there for too long—it just builds, until eventually I turn round to glare at her, tears running down my face. 'How *dare* you judge me? You're just like everyone else, disapproving of the fact that I'm obsessive then disapproving of the way I tried to pull myself out of it. Everyone's a fucking expert. But you know something Ruby? Sometimes there's nothing else you can do. Those drugs don't make you well—Jesus, they don't even make you feel better—but they turn off the static. The noise, the interference, the *shit* in your head that keeps you from understanding that you are destroying yourself.'

'You're smart,' Ruby says, looking at me anxiously because she knows I'm upset but she wants to stand her ground. 'You would have figured things out.'

'If we are going to be friends I need you to understand this. I'm smart but I *could not* figure things out. *Could not.* The worse things got, the more I called them destiny. By the end it was nothing to do with Michael. It was me. I wanted to believe that I could change how things ended by loving him hard enough. By loving him long enough. I wanted to finally keep a man, not have one leave like my fathers did, like they all do. To have some control over what a man does to me or perhaps what I mean is to want what a man does to me because in my experience they do it anyway.' The words start to catch in my throat, I'm starting to sob, I'm starting to repeat myself. 'I wanted to believe that love could change things.'

Ruby is touching me nervously, lightly, with the tips of her fingers. Her hand flits across my face, my arm. She is not sure if I will let her be near me and I am not sure either.

'It can change things,' she says. 'It does change things. Nothing you tell me, no argument we have, can change the fact I think you are,' she flounders for the right word, is insistent when she uses it. 'Lovely.'

'I was impossible,' I touch her hair, try to calm us both down. 'You have no idea how tedious and unremarkable madness can be.'

Travelling is like a night of heavy rain. It can clear away the heat and dust of the day, of all that has gone before. It can teach you how to be light, to let go. I wanted to drive, I was going to keep moving until I understood how I might do things differently.

I flew to Seattle and spent two nights on a houseboat. It rained, like everyone told me it would. I slept, sat watching the grey sky and grey water, and drank coffee. Then I hired a car and drove down to Portland. Along the way I stopped at one of many roadhouses with pro-gun posters and Vote One: Ollie North, though it was years since Ollie had stood for office.

'You travellin' alone?' the pump attendant asked. 'Kinda dangerous for a woman to be on her own around here.'

'I'm fine,' I said.

'Well excuse me for saying so ma'am, but you don't look fine.'

Great, I thought. Total strangers telling me I'm a wreck.

I stayed a night in Portland then drove through Salem and turned towards the coast. The roads were narrow and windy and small and I didn't know anything about where I was. It was pretty.

I stopped at Coos Bay, a fishing and tourist town with a plaque on the wall of the local restaurant commemorating a visit by John Kennedy. I slept in a cabin with a high double bed and a thick doona. It was cold even though it was the beginning of summer. A television was suspended from the ceiling above the bed and I watched 'Seinfeld' repeats. If I lowered my eyes I could see through the window and look out to sea. Moored boats rose gently with the ebb and flow of the tide.

I stopped again in Oregon and picked from the beach stones and shells polished by the sea. I slipped my thumb over their surface and they were so smooth it was like rubbing nothing at all. I carried one of the stones, a white quartz, for the rest of the journey. It's the stone I gave to you, Ruby.

By the time I hit northern California I was driving through fields of sunflowers. I lived on McDonald's. I didn't stop to eat; I used the drive-thrus and kept going, my foot hard on the accelerator, the countryside flickering past me. I played music at full blast.

In Monterey I visited the aquarium at Cannery Row and watched fish swoop and dive overhead like birds. I had always thought I'd come here with Michael, I had imagined driving this great American road with him. Instead my companion was a book, *By Grand Central Station I Lay Down and Wept*. During the days I drove, in the evening I read about a woman who became lovers with a married man in this part of California, a man who abandoned her after she had borne his four children. *I lean affirmation across the café table, and surrender my fifty years away with an easy smile.* When I reached Carmel and walked slowly through the Mission cloisters, I prayed to be saved from her fate.

I drove on to Big Sur, so I could visit Esalon. I could only get into the spa baths at one a.m. so I went to bed in my wooden cabin at nine o'clock then got up at twelve-thirty to drive the six miles to the baths. The night was quiet, bright. I was vague with sleep as I sat behind the wheel swinging with the curves, loose, as if I was on a motorbike. It was only when I was nearly there that I realised all the signs faced the other way and I was driving on the wrong side of the road. The thought filled me with pleasure, I embraced it, imagined a car bearing down on me, the impact as we collided. The slope into the sea was steep, I would roll ten, maybe twenty times. My seat belt would dig into me, it would cut me before it broke, releasing my body to be thrown through the windscreen onto the rocks. Gashed. Broken. There would be blood, my neck might break. It took an effort of will to stop these thoughts, to move to the other side of the road.

I walked through the paths of the beautifully manicured gardens, towards the lights on the cliffs where I knew the baths would be. At the cliffs I walked down a corridor until I came out in a kind of cave that was open to the Pacific Ocean. I got into the hot bath, heavy with minerals, and lay there. After half an hour or so I moved to the group spa, out in the open, on the edge of the cliff. The moon was low and bright, casting its cold light wide across the ocean. I lay there till nearly four o'clock, and watched the moon as it climbed the sky to sit directly over my head. *Moon, moon, rise in the sky to be a reminder of comfort and the hour when I was brave.*

The next day I drove on to Los Angeles but I kept having to stop by the road to watch sea otters playing in sea-forests of giant kelp. I was driven relentlessly down the coast of this country by desire, by longing. Finding instead of romance bigger things, better things. My head felt clear, my view larger. I escaped, for a moment, the endless self-absorption of a broken heart, the exhaustion of narcissism. I imagined that my aimless days of searching for love in the wrong places were drawing to a close. But it was more like this: in these days I understood for the first time that I could do things differently. It was more like the beginning of the end.

I arrived back in Sydney late at night and woke up, jetlagged, at six the next morning. When I walked down to the beach it was still dark except for the fishermen's lights scattered at intervals along the beach. I waded into the water, hoping the winter cold would wake me up. I was not paying attention but after a minute or two I looked at the shore and realised that it was moving away from me faster than it should have been. I was half asleep, it was dark, and I was caught in a rip. It shocked me, how quickly it happened, and for a moment I felt a surge of panic.

I knew what I had to do, Tony had lectured me endlessly on the subject. 'If you are ever caught in a rip, don't swim against the current—you will just exhaust yourself. Swim to the side of it, at a 45-degree angle. The rip won't be wide, they never are. And never overestimate your strength. Conserve it.' I was tempted, for a minute or so, to float out gently, to go with it, but Tony's words came to me and I began to swim at an angle to the shore.

When I got home I knocked on his bedroom door, not sure if he'd be there, but he was.

'You've woken me up. Go away.'

'It's seven o'clock already. You always get up around now, and besides, you haven't seen me for weeks. I need to thank you for the fact that you just saved my life, not fifteen minutes ago. I almost drowned.'

'My pleasure,' he said, as he rolled out of bed, looking bemused.

'So?' Tony asked, after I had told him about my road trip, 'Now you are both in town at the same time do you plan to see him?'

'I can't promise I won't. I've broken too many promises over the years. It seems safer not to make them.'

Tony nodded and sighed. 'I might have saved you this morning, Cath, in a virtual fashion. But I can't keep doing it. You're going to have to learn to save yourself. You do know that?'

'I know it,' I said. 'I just don't seem to be very good at it.'

Michael called. 'I came for a sabbatical. Can we have dinner? Please?' he asked. 'I need to talk to you.' So I betrayed myself, and my friends, and time, by letting all I had learnt slip away from me yet again. By walking down the same old street and leaping in that hole.

'Why did you fly out of Los Angeles the day I arrived?'

'Did I? I never knew when you planned on being in town.'

'I emailed,' I said. 'I left messages on your answering machine.'

'I never got the messages.'

'Right.'

'Believe what you want. Why would I lie about a thing like that?'

We met that evening at the Icebergs. Michael went to hug me but I pushed him away. While we sat and had a beer he stroked my arm, touched my face. If you'd been watching us from a distance you'd have thought we were happily reunited lovers. Once we'd finished a drink, before we'd ordered our second, he said this to me: 'I'm seeing someone else. I wanted to tell you in person. It isn't because she means more to me than you; it is because she's closer. It's the distance. It was impossible for us to keep going.' He talked to me slowly, with catch-up pauses, as if we were speaking on an international phone line.

'It was not impossible,' I said, after too long. 'It was only impossible because you made it so.'

All the while Michael kept telling me I looked beautiful. Kept touching me on the back of my hand, my cheek. Put his arm around me as we walked down the street to a restaurant. I didn't stop him, and I was frightened by my own passivity. After we ate—me all smiles and conversation—he walked me home and kissed me goodnight on the mouth in a way that suggested that nothing was over at all, not if I wanted to keep pushing, not if I was prepared to accept his terms. But instead I said goodnight and went up to the flat, alone.

When I got in the door I began to weep. I got into the bath still sobbing. My toes and fingers went white and wrinkly and I rocked back and forth in the water, moaning loudly. I didn't sound human. I was trying to melt away into the water, down the plughole, to disappear.

Through the haze, I became afraid of what I might do to myself. Tony was out. I was running out of people who could be bothered with this *thing*. Finally, I rang Marion in Melbourne, but I couldn't speak properly, made no sense.

'What is it, darling?' she asked, kept asking, but I just held onto the phone, not speaking.

'I am nothing,' I managed to say. 'I am falling in on myself.'

Tony came home. He knocked on the bathroom door but I was unable to answer, just kept on crying. He came in and stood by the bathtub, stared at me rocking.

'Get out, baby.'

'I thought you were staying out tonight,' I sobbed.

'I was. Marion rang me. She was worried about what you might do to yourself. This has to stop. Catherine, how do we make you stop?'

'I'm sorry,' I sobbed. 'I'm sorry.'

'Stop apologising.' He leant over me and pulled me up by the armpits as if I was a child. 'Put this towel around you.' He tucked me into bed and then made me a cup of tea. 'There is lots of sugar in this,' he said. Then, 'Can I snuggle in with you?'

I hesitated. 'For old time's sake,' he said after a few moments of silence.

'Yes, please.' He pulled off his trousers, crawled in and put his arms around me.

'He is finally treating me like a girlfriend now it's over,' I told him. 'It makes no sense.'

'It makes sense,' Tony said. 'Sex and emotional connection together overwhelm him. He can only do one at a time. But frankly I don't care if it makes sense or not. I just want him to stop contacting you. Or you to get the strength to stop seeing him. You have to learn to care enough about yourself. And your friends.'

Tony held me for a while.

'I've broken my own rule,' I said finally.

'What rule is that?'

'The five-year rule. If you are obsessing about a situation after five years it's crossed the line.'

'A five-month rule would be better,' said Tony.

Still I kept seeing him, convincing myself that not sleeping with him counted as looking after myself. If my friends expressed concern, I simply lied to them about what I was up to.

I believed I was keeping it together. My life might sometimes look like it was unravelling but I was managing, I thought, to hold on to most of the threads. One night I drove us to dinner in Darlinghurst and turned the wrong way down a one-way street, then almost crashed the car when I parked it.

'Good park,' Michael laughed. 'You seem a bit wired tonight.' Then, when we were sitting in the restaurant, 'You look incredible.'

I was wearing a tight shirt that showed lots of cleavage. I had hoped that might make me feel powerful, but it didn't, it filled me with contempt. For both of us. I look back on things and I realise that I spent years not wanting to admit how shallow men can be. That people can declare true love, that churches can be formed, that fathers can leave their flesh and blood, for nothing more than this—a good pair of tits.

'Are you trying to make things hard for me?' Michael asked, 'By dressing like that?'

I look at him and imagine smashing my glass of wine in his face, cutting him up, blinding him, making him bleed. I imagine slashing myself. I look at my arms and imagine the glass going in.

'I miss you,' Michael is saying. 'I always miss you, that's what I can't bear about this.'

I am trapped in a bad play, the lines not convincing even to me, who wants desperately to be convinced. I drop Michael off where he is staying and he gets out of the car.

He hesitates, stands by the car, drums his fingers on the roof, then leans back in and kisses me all over my face, on the mouth. I think he will leave it at that but he doesn't, begins to bite my lips hard, my neck.

He drops to his knees on the pavement beside the car. He put his head in my lap. He is shaking.

'You have to let go of me,' he says.

'You say, on your knees, kneeling before me.'

He doesn't answer, but puts his hands on my breasts, buries his face into my lap, breathes me in.

'I love your smell,' he says, as he has said many times over the years. 'We are right for each other.'

I get out of the car and push him against it, keep kissing him while he puts one hand under my shirt, undoes my jeans with the other. He turns us around so now I'm against the car, he puts two fingers in my cunt, one in my arse, my hand reaches back for his cock. He bites me so hard he draws blood. We strain and push against each other, like we are wrestling.

He pulls back, 'It is important to me that you understand,' he says, 'why we can't see each other any more.' I don't understand, refuse to even now and we end up clawing at each other, half-hitting, half-embracing.

I want you to kill me, I think. I want to die.

As if he hears me, Michael reaches out and puts both hands around my throat so tight it hurts. He shakes me slowly. He shakes me with force.

'We. Must. Stop. This.' He lets go of my throat, pushes

me hard away from him. 'We are driving each other crazy.'

He walks off, breathing sharply, retching air. I'm left alone in the driveway, and even though there is no one to see me now I slide down the side of the car to the ground. That is the role I have chosen. I am the victim. I will always be hurt and left. I don't know any other way. I pull myself onto all fours and bang my forehead over and over onto the asphalt until finally, to my relief, I gash myself. I sit quietly there on the concrete and bleed tears down my face.

I look back at this and I can see it is not that exciting. A long night in the bath and waterlogged skin. Bored friends. A fantasy of drowning, of crashing my car, ripping my own flesh open with metal, slicing up Michael's flesh with glass. I'd like to make it seem like there was more drama. But the point of my story is how quietly you can lose years. How gently they can slip away from you. You can spend so much time waiting for something to happen, and then…well, it simply doesn't.

When I was reading all those classics at university, about heroines like Jane Eyre and Anna Karenina, I'd rail against the times that reduced women to such dependence, though for all my travelling, my working, my friendships, I too had spent years hanging around waiting for someone, some *man*, to fix everything up. From the outside it didn't look like that, not that you'd know it from the story I'm telling. From the outside I had a good job, I was a success,

I looked sexy. I was smart and funny. Etcetera. All the positive things we tell ourselves and each other to make it all seem okay. I call myself a feminist. But this is my secret, many women's secret: there is a darkness in me that isn't about how kinky I can get in bed, or the rage I often feel. In fact 'darkness' is the wrong word. 'Beige' is more the word to describe the passivity that eats away at me, away at us, but seems like nothing at all.

The books I read were full of warnings it took me too long to heed. I read them for romance but now I see they were written to save women like me from ourselves. Don't wait, that is what I say to people now. Never wait. I am a born-again on this subject. What do the Nike ads say? Just Do It. I offer up my childlessness as my scar.

Twelve

We stand on the Indira Gandhi Bridge, which is some two kilometres long and connects Rameshwaram to India's mainland. We are both subdued. I'm exhausted by the intensity of our recent discussions. Ever since our argument after the temple I've remembered more of what happened to me with Laura's dad and more of the shit I took from Michael. More of the terrible distress I felt when my first father, then my dad, left me. The low-level grief I've felt for years has been washed away by the rage that is swamping me. I'm feeling things the way everyone has always said I should, and I do not like it. I don't like it at all.

I wonder if it would be best if Ruby and I part. I don't want to fight with her, and I don't want to dump this on her either. But I'm shying away from the thought of not being with her. I am starting to understand what this might mean and am becoming frightened.

Ruby is pointing at Adam's Bridge, the scattering of

tiny islands and boulders that stretch from here to Sri Lanka, twenty-two kilometres away. It is very beautiful where blue sea meets a blue sky striped with streaky white clouds, the sand and green of Rameshwaram directly below.

'The Tamil Tigers want to build a real bridge across Adam's Bridge between Jaffna and here,' I say. 'There are lots of Tamil refugees living on this island and back on the mainland—they want to hook up.'

'It shouldn't be called Adam's Bridge,' Ruby says. 'That's Christian colonisation talking. It's Hanuman's Bridge if it's anyone's. In the *Ramayana* Hanuman, Rama's faithful helper, ran over these stones searching for Rama's wife, Sita. She had been kidnapped by Ravana, demon-king of Ceylon. It was a battle of two of life's great forces: Ravana is a devotee of Siva the Destroyer and Rama is an incarnation of Vishnu, the Preserver.

'And you may laugh, Catherine,' Ruby goes on, school-marmish. If she wore spectacles she'd be looking at me over the top of them. 'But I think you have lived in the thrall of Siva, with your fixation on catastrophe, sex and disasters. I'd recommend a stint of Brahma worship—even Vishnu is too in-the-head for you, with all that emphasis on dreams.'

I smile at her, but, as happens so often with Ruby at the moment, I don't know what to say. It is hot, she is sweating and I run a hand over her head, where there is now enough hair to show a hint of curl.

We get back in the hire car and drive to the main village, about ten kilometres further along. When we arrive we find a strange and sandy place. People come here to worship Vishnu but the Ramalingeshwara Temple is closed when we get there, leaving us with only the famous colonnades to walk through. Their length—205 metres—is impressive but the columns themselves are concrete copies of what was once there. It is only when we walk past the ruins of the original columns, looking like so many fallen giants, that we understand what this place must once have been.

We walk through the heat to the water, past the shops that sell objects made of shells, strings of shells, macramé and shells.

'What will you do when you get back to Melbourne?' I ask.

'I'm still interested in aid organisations,' she says. 'I'd like to make a career of it but I'm not sure if that means going back to uni to do development studies or applying for every job going. Probably both. You?'

'Well, I think I'm back in Melbourne for good now. I figured I couldn't base a whole life on good weather patterns and surf. I've gone back to writing, do a bit of consulting for extra cash. So I guess I'll just keep going along the same—new—track.'

'You will keep in touch, won't you?' Ruby asks, anxious. 'I know we've been fighting. I know it has been a bit difficult. You won't suddenly decide I'm too young once you are back among your old—emphasis on old—friends?'

I put my arm around her shoulder, pulling her close. 'We won't lose touch,' I say. 'You are my new and most favourite friend.'

We walk past the sadhus; wild dreadlocked men with orange cloths round their waists. One of them looks at us lustfully, pointedly. Then we see a naked sadhu, covered from head to foot in white ash, supposedly from funeral pyres, Ruby tells me.

This place is lighter than Land's End and Kanniya-kumari. The atmosphere is less commercial, more fun. We sit and watch the women in their colourful saris, the businessmen who strip down to their underpants before wading in, the priests picnicking on the ghats that lead down to the water. Cows wander, down there by the sea, sniffing gently at people's food. Everyone is hanging out, killing time until the temple reopens at five p.m. and they can go and get their blessing.

'Have you read *All's Well that Ends Well*?' Ruby asks me as we sit on the ghats and watch the sun go down. I am bemused.

'No,' I say.

'There is this quote from it,' she says. '*I am undone: there is no living, none, / If Bertram be away. 'Twere all one / That I should love a bright particular star / And think to wed it, he is so above me: / In his bright radiance and collateral light / Must I be comforted, not in his sphere. / The ambition in my love thus plagues itself.*

'That's you,' she goes on. 'It was the ambition in your love that plagued you.'

I look at her, surprised. 'That's it exactly,' I say. 'When I was at my lowest I felt undone.'

Tony was home for a Sunday of domestic duties. I missed him now that he was hardly here and it was good to see him, despite the fact that on this particular day he was so scratchy and irritable.

'It's the full moon,' I laughed. 'My period's due. Perhaps we're cycling.'

'Well, how come you're in such a good mood?'

'I'm through the monthly suicidal days. The happy hormones have started.' And it was true. I was full of joy, light-headed with it. As madly up as I had been down.

That night I woke up nauseous, back aching, and tried to walk to the bathroom. Dizziness hit me halfway so I dropped to my knees and crawled. By the time I got to the bathroom I was sweating and all I wanted to do was lie on the cold, smooth tiles, feel the cool of them against my cheek. I lay like that for two hours, half conscious, until Tony found me at six a.m.

'Jesus,' he said, helping me up. A few minutes later he was sitting by me in bed, wiping my brow with a washer. 'Go to the doctor, all right? Today.'

'Lots of women have bad periods.'

'This is beyond bad. That's the problem with you women, you're natural masochists. You lose all sense of what is reasonable pain.'

I went to my GP. She booked me in for an ultrasound and the next thing I knew I was in stirrups while a woman in a twin set and pearls inserted a large camera-tipped phallus into me. This was not how I'd imagined being here, in this place that pregnant women come to see their unborn babies for the first time, in this place where the receptionist asked, 'How many months?' before she realised I was ill, not with child. Fairly quickly the ultrasound found a growth the size of a grapefruit. Then a second one.

My stomach bloats. My bladder feels full, I piss all the time. I am nauseous, I am in pain, I am mad—a hormonal punching bag, out of control. The object in my stomach grows larger by the week. I cannot roll on my stomach because it hurts. I am giving birth to a deformity, a growth, a shadow: a shadow child to my shadow lover.

The doctor said that after the operation I might be infertile. For years I have been dreaming my little girl. She is not born yet, but I know her. She is a wild child with curls and a sticky-out tummy. She is full of bad behaviour. She is waiting for me, waiting for me to be ready to let her be born. I am scared that if I do not have a child of my own, I will never grow up, that I will die gazing at myself in the water's reflection.

I cannot sleep. Instead of counting sheep, I chant the names of the football clubs, the twelve that were around when I was growing up: Carlton, Collingwood, Richmond, Essendon, North Melbourne, South Melbourne, Hawthorn, Footscray, Fitzroy, Geelong, St Kilda, Melbourne. If I'm not asleep by then I move on to the new list: Port Adelaide, the Crows, West Coast Eagles, Bulldogs, Fremantle Dockers, Sydney Swans, Brisbane Lions, Carlton, Collingwood, Richmond, Essendon, Kangaroos, Hawthorn, Geelong, St Kilda, Melbourne. This second list is harder. The names have less to do with places; I don't know where these teams are from. Melbourne is slipping away from me. In this, and other things. The summers have been hot since I left; the city is in drought. It is true, I think, the rain does follow me. This thought jolts me awake and I brood on the weather, how I no longer live where it is hot, how where I am is always cold.

A month later I was lying in surgery while an anaesthetist placed a drip in my arm. 'Think of a nice place,' he said. 'Of somewhere that makes you happy.' I panicked. Where would that nice place be, what nice place?

Then I was waking and calling out to my mother who had flown from Adelaide to be with me, who was sitting beside me, holding my hand and telling me she loved me. I began calling for Michael, even though we had not been in contact for a year, even though I could barely remember what he looked like any more. Calling out his name, over and over.

The morphine made me drowsy and floaty. I left the television on and dozed on and off against a background of footage of emergency workers digging bodies from the mudslide at Thredbo. Resorts and apartments had slipped forward and crumpled, piling house upon house and leaving a gash across the landscape. Drugged as I was, it truly seemed a miracle to me when Stuart Diver was pulled out of the earth some 68 hours later, his tortured face blinking at the light.

When I couldn't focus on the screen I would lie for hours listening to Joni Mitchell's *Blue*, her songs of travel and love and blood. *I could drink a case of you, darling / And I would still be on my feet.*

I was not on my feet. After days of not getting better the doctor decided I was anaemic because of the blood I had lost in surgery. I had painfully, slowly, given litres of my own blood in the weeks before the operation. Now they slowly dripped it back into me.

The day I got home I stood in the mirror and looked at myself. The scar red, raw and not yet joined, the shaving rash, the uneven mix of stubble and pubic hair, and the blisters caused by an allergic reaction to the surgical tape. There were bruises on my belly, on my pubis. All that had been lush now devastated. It was impossible to imagine the regrowth. It was impossible to imagine that anyone would love me in my ugliness.

Tony made sure I had meals cooked for me when I got out of hospital, but he always went back to his girlfriend's to sleep. It was a lonely time. I'd been out of hospital three weeks when Michael called. 'I'm in town for ten days or so. I didn't know whether you would want me to call. Are you up to visitors? I heard you've been sick.'

'Sure,' I said. 'Come over.'

I was nervous and when I answered the door I could see he was too. He looked old. Not sexy old, but old old. That made sense, I realised, he was well into his fifties now, but this was the first time he had struck me that way. Even his eyes had lost their intensity and seemed a paler blue. The lines on his face were drooping into folds. It looked like his confidence had evaporated, leaving him deflated. He looked like a man who had given up. I suppose I looked pretty much like a woman who had given up as well.

'You look great in pyjamas,' he kissed me, handing over some flowers. 'I don't think I've ever seen you in nightwear before. There was never the need.' He smiled at me. 'Have you lost weight?'

We talked, and were polite to each other, and after an hour I asked him to leave because I was tired. A few days later he came by again. He cooked me a meal while I lay on the couch watching the coverage of Princess Diana's death. I could not turn off the TV and the stories of shattered bodies dripped into me, like the stories of the dead at

Thredbo, like the blood I had needed. I was like Gollum, feeding off the misery of others, shrinking, twisting into deformity. Trevor Rees-Jones, Diana's bodyguard, had a smashed up face and had bitten off part of his tongue. I kept thinking about that. The fact that he bit off his own tongue.

'Since when did you become a royalist?' Michael asked, coming in to sit beside me on the couch.

'I'm not one,' I said. 'But no one expects a princess to have such a grisly end. *Sleeping Beauty* was my favourite fairytale when I was a kid. She was meant to be woken from a long slumber when a prince kissed her. She was meant to get married and live happily ever after.'

'She'd already divorced Charles, been bulimic and had lovers while she was still with Charles, who was on with Camilla Parker-Bowles. You call that a fairy tale?' Then he stopped himself launching into a lecture and tried to soften. He put his arm around me and hugged me. 'Actually, I'm upset, too,' he said, 'and I don't know why, either.'

As I sat watching the television that night, cuddled up to Michael, I realised it was true. I had believed in fairy tales. Yet here I was, watching the flowers pile up outside Kensington Palace with a man who couldn't love me on the couch beside me.

That night I dreamt that it was my chest that had been cut open, not my abdomen, my heart was ripped and bleeding, just as Diana's had been. I woke with a start, pain pulling my chest tight, unable to breathe.

*

'Where's your flatmate?' Michael asked when he came around again the next night. 'He never seems to be here.'

'At his girlfriend's.'

'I thought he was your boyfriend. I get some of the gossip over in Los Angeles, you know.'

'He was a kind of boyfriend, but now he's just a good friend. Anyway, he's started seeing someone else.'

'Are you jealous?'

'Yes, actually.'

'Have you been seeing anyone?' he asked.

'Do I look like I could be dating anyone?' I gestured down.

The conversation was stilted and awkward. I didn't want to talk about these things with him. I did not want to tell Michael that I had had lovers but that things always ended because whenever they touched me I thought of him. I didn't tell him that I had known he was in town because I had dreamt he was here and then a friend had rung me up the very next morning to tell me. I didn't say that I dreamt of him often. That I always felt I knew where in the world he was, and whether he was with someone else. When people would tell me what he was up to, it would seem I had been right, that my dreams were prophetic. I didn't talk to anyone about any of this any more. I knew it was mad. I couldn't even see what it was I had found attractive in him. I treated him like some kind of altar upon which I was compelled to sacrifice myself.

'I leave in two days.' He stroked my face. 'I can't stop thinking about you. Please? Can you? Can we?' He dropped his face to my belly, kissing it gently all over. Undoing the drawstring of my pyjamas, kissing my scar in all its ugliness, tracing my bruising with his tongue. I was afraid.

'The doctor said I should wait at least six weeks,' I whispered.

'We can't wait. I'll be gone by then.' Michael moaned into my ear. Despite, or because of, the danger of unhealed wounds, of lost blood, of pain, I let him inside me. He moved cautiously at first, 'Is this okay?' he murmured, 'I'll take the weight with my arms,' and within a second I came. The intensity of my orgasm was frightening, it racked me, it hurt me, but I couldn't stop moving against him and had to bite my tongue to stop myself saying 'I love you.' Even though I didn't, even though I didn't love him. I did not stop him when he seemed to forget I was ill and pushed into me too hard, bit me. In one place he drew blood and all over I could feel the bruises bloom.

Afterwards, as we lay together he stroked my hair. He was tense. There were a few silent minutes then he said, 'You should know something. That woman I was seeing in Los Angeles last year. We broke up but then got together again three months ago. I'm serious about her.'

In old-fashioned novels I'd have had the vapours or maybe a seizure. Perhaps, like Mademoiselle Tourvel, I'd simply have lain down and died. But in the ungainly jargon of the nineties, it seemed I was having an anxiety attack. I struggled for air while my limbs twitched uncontrollably. I was a dying animal. I was road kill. Michael had never seen me like this before, and glanced anxiously at the door.

'I'm sorry,' he said. 'My timing could have been better.' He tried to kiss me, but I was not there to be kissed. I was nowhere.

'I'm sorry,' he said again, leaning down to touch my face before he left. But I moved slightly to avoid him—it wasn't hard—and then he was gone.

As awful as that night was, I had seen it coming. I had behaved out of habit. 'Stage four,' I told Tony when I saw him next. 'I know the hole is there. I'm thinking that soon now, I might be able walk around it.'

As I recovered I began to walk around the cliffs again each morning. No matter how I felt, the walk always sustained me. One morning as I stepped outside my flat I saw a little boy from one of the tourist buses run across the road in front of me and trip in front of an oncoming car. The jolt of adrenalin that surged through my body was electrifying and I moved faster than I ever had before, despite the surgery. I didn't feel any pain. Out of the corner of my eye—my peripheral vision seemed to have increased supernaturally—I saw the pavement full of coffee drinkers rise as if they were part of an action replay. Colours were intense.

I swooped on the boy, pulling him out of the way, half expecting him to push me away in angry fright, but he collapsed into my arms, sobbing in terror, and I carried him to the side of the road. Even though my doctors had said not to lift anything, even though I had been too weak to lift anything for months. The mother came running out of the café, yelling at him in her fear. I left them and walked down to the sea as the adrenalin flood ebbed away. For days I was jittery with the chemicals pumping through my system.

And finally it was chemicals that saved me. There were the ones the doctor gave me which at first made me sleepless and manic but, over the weeks, less anxious and more relaxed. Then there were the ones my body made when I swam and walked each day.

Bad chemistry, I used to think, had taken me to Michael and convinced me he was the one. Now it was chemistry that gave me the strength to loosen my grip, begin to let go.

Thirteen

We walk past hessian bags with pink jasmine falling out, past yellow and orange marigolds being weighed on scales and white tubular flowers that smell like gardenias. The flowers' fragrance is strong in this market, as is the smell of their rotting blooms. There is none of the order we saw outside Buddhist temples in Sri Lanka where lotuses were laid out in neat rows and frangipani arranged in the shape of bodhi leaves.

The humidity is bad enough outside; in here it is so dense we are moving through a hot fog. I yearn for rain; we are all yearning for rain. We are all of us rank with sweat, surrounded by flowers, by people pressing up against us, we hold our bags tightly to our side, avert our faces from the hands that are grabbing at our earrings. Everything tumbles, everywhere it is chaotic.

We get to the other side of the market, out into the open air, and Ruby beams at me, sweat beading on her forehead. 'Unreal,' she says. 'That was the best place we've been since we arrived in India.'

We cross the road from the market to one of the temple complexes. It is so vast it is more like a town than a temple. I see one of the temple elephants chained up in a doorway. He is very old. He has large round white symbols painted around his eyes and orange circles on his sides. I hold out a coin and he delicately picks it off my palm with his trunk. Then he places his trunk, thick as a man's thigh, on my head with a delicate thud.

'I love that elephant,' I say. 'I *love* it. Is it bad luck to go for a second blessing?'

'It's greedy,' Ruby says. 'Let other people have their blessings. What was your wish?'

'That it rain.' I say. Then it happens. We hear a noise above us. It grows steadily louder and louder and we realise it is the sound of rain. We race outside into the deluge. The weather has finally broken and the physical relief is enormous. We burst out laughing and hug each other.

'It's a miracle,' Ruby says. 'You are a *goddess*.'

I have never encountered such rain; you cannot see more than two inches in front of you. The streets of Madurai flood within minutes.

The city's twelve temples, some forty-six metres high, all centuries old, have sheets of water running down their sides. There are hundreds of thousands of sculptures and I think of them now, the gods and goddesses and animal kings being cleansed by the waterfall. The flower sellers in the courtyard are soaked, their necklaces of flowers destroyed. People wade through the muck. Kids dance around in the rain holding hands. The betchak drivers careen past touting for fares, but it is clear they will be stopped in their tracks before long.

'It is chaos,' says Ruby. 'We can't walk. We can't get anywhere.'

We run into the tailor market, where rows of tailors sew bolts of bright coloured cloth into trousers and shirts. They are watched over by large stone Ganesas and Kalis, both garlanded with bright flowers and blackened with age and the butter that pilgrims rub into the stone. This market was once a temple. It sits lower than the street, so now water is gushing into it and the traders are hesitating, trying to decide whether to pack up or keep going. We stand with water up to our ankles, looking at packets of bindis, rows of coloured bangles and trays of gold earrings.

The woman behind the counter nods at me, then to Kali behind me. 'You want a child,' she says. 'You should pray to her. I will pray for you as well. Perhaps it's not too late.'

I'm taken aback, I'm not sure if Ruby has heard us. Either way, she distracts us both. 'How much are these?' says Ruby, who is fingering rows of glass bangles in dark reds and blues and gold. 'How do I put them on?'

'You must push, very hard,' the old woman takes Ruby's arm and, without asking, rubs it with oil. 'Hold your hand like this,' she demonstrates, holding her own hand in a beak, then takes Ruby's hand and squeezes it so her thumb is tight against the palm. 'Now it must be hurting,' she says and she forces the bangles in lots of four over Ruby's knuckles and onto her arm.

Ruby's forearm, it seems to be made of glass, it is so delicate. 'How do I get them off?' she asks.

'When their time is up they will break and fall. To hurry them along is very bad luck. You will have these bangles on your arm for some years now.' She smiles at Ruby, Ruby smiles back.

We hesitate, look again at the downpour. 'Madam must also be having some bangles,' says the stall owner who, like us, is now shin deep in water. She grabs my wrist. 'Madam wants me to pray for her doesn't she? Otherwise she will have no children.' I pull away, grimacing.

'Let's run to that café next door.' Ruby points three doors down, her arm tinkling as she moves.

We run. It is hard to see where we are going but we make it to the café. 'That crone freaked me out,' I say when we get inside.

'Yes, she does have a touch of evil.' Then we both laugh like small children who have escaped from an imaginary witch. Ruby shakes herself off and I can hear the sound of her bangles as she moves. 'She isn't all bad luck,' I say. 'It's like you're wearing a cat bell. I'll always know where you are.'

'Meow,' she says, stretching, theatrically feline. 'I am your pussycat.' She licks her arm, the one without bangles on it, from the inside of her wrist along the blue vein to that soft place behind her elbow.

I would like to pretend I never saw Michael again but that is not how it happened. I didn't contact him for six months or so after he left that last time, but he kept writing little notes to me, some of them apologetic, some conversational, and one day I answered. I can't even remember why. The number of emails that passed between us went up to three and four a day.

'I'm a bit old for it, I know, but think I might be having some kind of mid-life crisis,' he wrote. 'You are one of the few people I can talk to about things.'

We emailed each other as he drove up the west coast of the States. That was something I had always dreamed we would do together, and I suppose we did, in the end. Him driving, breaking down literally, breaking down metaphorically. Me typing, imagining it all in my head. But this time the endless writing to each other felt different. I would circle an idea, a thought, pacing around my apartment, my computer, before I caught the moment where the right words came to me. It was as if this circling and waiting, this learning when to strike, helped me understand not just the movement of ideas and language, but of life and how to move on with it. I understood that I had been circling Michael too long and it made me feel freer to be his friend.

It was a time of storms. In the winter the whole of northeast America had been brought to a halt by ice storms. Beautiful at first, dangerous at last; three thousand miles of power lines were crumpled and crushed by the layers of ice that had built up slowly over several days until the pylons, and much of Canada, had been beaten to their knees. That summer California was assaulted as well. 'It is raining,' Michael wrote. 'It is flooding. I'm stuck outside of Big Sur with nowhere to stay. I have found a bar to hide in, but it looks as if I'll be sleeping in the car tonight. The road is collapsing. Sometimes I think I am collapsing too. I feel as if I am drowning.'

So much water. By the end there was only water.

'If you think you are drowning,' I replied, 'imagine that I am there beside you, holding your head up so you can breathe.' Despite the fact that he had spent the last few years in that state of panic drowning can induce, grabbing at me when he was desperate, almost taking me down with him.

That Christmas Michael came back to Sydney to see his family, as he always did.

'Are you nervous about seeing me?' I wrote.

'Maybe,' he answered. 'A bit. We can cross that bridge when we come to it.'

He asked me to a Christmas party but then was uncomfortable having me in the room. He spent much of the night talking to women who flirted with him, their hands placed flat and proprietorial on his chest as they talked intensely to him. I wondered if they thought, like I had once, that they were special to him. As I watched him that night he at last seemed ordinary to me. As he had got older he had become thinner, frailer and that was how he seemed: insubstantial, feeding off women's admiration in an attempt to fuel himself, puff himself up.

I felt light. His dismissiveness didn't hurt. I had expected it, I realised, because in our final emails we had finally developed a real intimacy, and that was something he could never abide. The betrayal of our last months of friendship finally made me lose all respect for him. This is something I did come to understand over those years. That friendship was the most important thing of all.

I left the party early and he saw me out then tried to kiss me. I turned away from him. 'Can I come by tomorrow night?' he asked and I said yes. There was something I needed to do.

After he arrived at my flat the next evening we went for a walk on the beach. 'I have offered again and again to come to Los Angeles and you have never told me why you didn't want me to come,' I said.

'That's a bit intense, isn't it?' he said.

'I don't even want to any more,' I said, 'I just want you to answer the question I've been asking for years. Why didn't you want me to come to Los Angeles?'

He cocked his head, quoted Hemingway. *'Oh Jake, we could have had such a damned good time together.'*

And at that moment I saw clearly what others had seen for years, what Michael himself had told me more than once—that he was incapable. The relief, of seeing clearly, of understanding, washed over me like a wave of joy.

He sat staring at the water for a time. 'You know, whenever I'm sitting at Bondi at night, looking across to the lights on the other side of the bay, I feel sad.' He turned back to me. 'I suppose that doesn't answer your question.'

I slept with him that night, to see if it was true, that I had been released, and it was. So many times when I had been with other men, or simply talking to friends, living my life, I had drifted off into another world, the world where Michael and I made love. Now that I was with him I just wanted to be alone, with the sound of the surf.

At one point he moved up behind me, crossed his arms around my breasts and pulled me towards him, kissing the back of my neck. A moment while he slept when he was tender. I lay there and felt his heartbeat, and his breath, against my back. I watched as the sea mist coiled in through my window like a fat white snake. It comforted me, the solidity of the air here, in this suburb I loved. It was practically stroking me.

There was a morning two weeks later when the sky was heavy and grey, the water the colour of steel. It was cold on the beach, not like summer at all. It was a relief to dive into water that was warmer than air and I cut through the Bondi surf as quickly as possible so I could warm up. I swam to the Icebergs then back again. Just as I was about to enter the rock pool and get out of the water Michael swam past me in the other direction. If I'd reached out I could have touched him. He moved through my space, past me, as I had so often dreamt him doing. It was as if I was dreaming him still. Back on the land, where the light was hard and things were solid, I never saw him again.

So that is my story. Water runs through it. So do dreams and seasons and light. There is Hollywood and blood; once, twice, many times. There is family and friends. 'Seinfeld' ended shortly before the last time I slept with Michael and the last episode was, appropriately, a disappointment. There are beatings and police, earthquakes and fires and, at the end, the death of a princess. There is the World Wide Web and planes connecting lovers and family together. There is also the fantasy that we live in a global village and distance makes no difference. It does make a difference, I learnt. Distance makes all the difference in the world.

What I can say is, 'This is what happened to me in the nineties.' I suspect that some of the things that happened to me are not so different from things that happened to other people. My story is neat in another way as well. There is a wedding. Just like in all those novels I used to read.

'Catherine?' Finn called me around ten p.m. I was up, watching the news. It was the night of the Sydney hailstorms on April 19, 1999. I was to find out later that they destroyed twenty-eight thousand house roofs and sixty thousand cars. Not that I knew all the statistics when Finn rang. All I knew then was it had started with a sound like thunder that built to a roar. The roar engulfed the flat, the suburb and the city, as hail clattered and smashed into metal and asphalt and tiles. After it was over I ran outside, along with everyone else, to see piles of hail-stones the size of tennis balls and bigger.

'Guess what?' I said. 'There has been this amazing hailstorm that's practically wiped out the city. Hail the size of footballs. I've never seen anything like it.'

'I rang *you*,' Finn said. 'It's me that gets to say "Guess what?" Any damage?'

'Not to me.'

'Good,' he paused. 'Guess what? Anna and I are getting married in July. I want you to be my best man.'

The gathering of the clans was held on a rooftop in Manhattan. For both Finn and Anna it was the first time their scattered and various families had come together in the one space. There were mothers and fathers, brothers and sisters, stepfathers and mothers, half-brothers and stepsisters. My mother flew in from Adelaide with her third husband and one of his four daughters. My first father travelled from Paris with his second wife and three sons. My second father came in from Bangkok, with his third wife and her children.

Anna's parents had divorced some years before and they paced opposite sides of the rooftop, eyeing each other warily. Anna's sisters had come from Chicago and Los Angeles. Her Italian relatives on her father's side were all there, enjoying themselves despite the unconventional nature of the affair. Food was piled metres high: fresh salmon and salads, chicken, caviar and beef. There were cakes, pastries and melted chocolate to dip the strawberries in, strawberries that were as large as mandarins, but sweet, none the less. It was a hot evening but just before the guests arrived buckets of rose petals were strewn on the concrete. Finn's contribution had been to place waratah—God knows where he found them—at regular intervals along the roof wall.

I had never seen Finn so nervous. I stood by him as he waited for Anna to arrive. 'Do you think I'm mad?' he asked. 'To do this surrounded by the wreckage of so many marriages?'

'Not mad. Brave. You two are right for each other. You have taken longer to make your choice than these guys did first time around. You're practically ancient compared to all of them when they first got married.'

'Less ancient than you. And less fat.'

'But so much more mature.' I kissed him.

The ceremony was simple and afterwards there were

speeches. We all had our turn and when I had mine I read
a poem by Raymond Carver:

> *And did you get what*
> *You wanted from this life, even so?*
> *I did.*
> *And what did you want?*
> *To call myself beloved, to feel myself*
> *Beloved on the earth.*

It was the solstice and the twilight lasted till after ten. Once
it got dark we lit tea light candles between the waratahs.
Everyone began to dance drunkenly, as they always do at
the end of weddings. That part of the evening is inevitable
and awkward, but as I watched my family moving among
and around each other I felt a certain pride that despite
living all over the world, despite history, we had all known
this was important. Had all managed to be here, in this one
place at the one time to watch Finn build a family of his
own. It was that night I decided to move back to Melbourne.
To move closer to the people that loved me most.

'It took so long,' Ruby sighs melodramatically. Taunting
me. 'I thought grownups got smarter.'

'People do learn as they get older,' I reply. 'It just
always, always, takes longer than you'd like.'

'Anyway, it's a happy ending,' Ruby says. She is lying on her back, on the bed, arms spread out. 'With the wedding, and sense of resolution and so forth.'

'Yes.'

It has been a long day, what with wading back to our hotel to find it was sodden, then moving our things to a hotel that hadn't flooded. The rain has receded, leaving Madurai like a steam bath.

We are lying together on a king-size bed in the luxury of our new airconditioned hotel. It has cable television and we have BBC news on in the background. It is the first time I've watched television in three months, and three months is the longest time I've been away from it for fifteen years.

'So what stage are you at now?' Ruby asks.

'Stage four,' I say. 'I walk around the hole.'

'You mean you don't have sex,' Ruby laughs.

She's right. I've avoided it for more than two years now.

'You've got to get to stage five,' Ruby says, doing her theatrical thing, talking to me in an even, pleasant voice, like some kind of new-age guru. 'You've got to walk down a different street.'

'You're a dork,' I say. I look at the cable channel guide. 'Let's watch *Groundhog Day*. It'll be my eighth time.'

'It's an old film, isn't it?' Ruby says. '1993?'

'1993 is not old,' I say.

'In seven years every cell in your body has regenerated,'

Ruby says. 'There is not one part of you that is around now that you had in '93. Not one little cell or one bit of mitochondria. Cool, huh?'

'Cool.'

We both turn back to the TV. 'Look at that,' we both say at once, because the image on the screen doesn't make sense. One of the towers of the World Trade Center is on fire and the other has a plane heading straight towards it.

'That looks bad,' she says.

'It does. But there is a world of time for bad news and we are only travelling together for a short time more. Let's turn off the TV.'

We do. Ruby swigs on her beer. 'Do you still love Michael?'

'He's just a story now. Some things I've told you probably aren't even true, you know what memory does to things.'

'So, is there room for someone else?' Ruby asks.

'There is room,' I say, my chest feeling tight. I've wanted this conversation but now I can feel my panic descending. I need time to think. More time.

'Would it ruin your story if you found love again?' Ruby rolls from her back onto her stomach, wriggles towards me on the bed. She puts her head on her arms and looks at me and it is like the two of us are lying beside each other on a towel on a beach on a hot Bondi day. She smiles at me, mischievous.

'You're flirting,' I say. 'And I think my story's

narrative structure requires me to stay single.'

'I know we clash,' she goes on, 'but the way I see it we rub up against each other because we spark.' She pauses for breath, a bit nervous. 'So, would it really ruin your story,' she repeats, 'if you fell in love with a friend? Would people say you had sold out by giving the heroine a person to make her even happier? Rather than allowing her to struggle on, independently, bravely, having found herself etcetera etcetera.'

'I suppose I could live with their disappointment,' I say after a while, in a sweat.

She smiles at me again, teasing. 'I could teach you those things we talked about at dinner that time. Sexy lesbian things. Those things you couldn't imagine.'

Suddenly I am having no problem with my imagination at all. I imagine my fingers inside her, the intense heat of her, the way her cunt clenches at my hand as if she wants to take me all in. I imagine how very wet she is and how silky that feels. Thinking of this, I am beside myself. I am in myself.

She is so close now that we are almost kissing, and I find that I am having trouble thinking of saying anything to her, of doing anything but kissing her. So that's what I do. I lean forward towards my beautiful friend, my gorgeous friend, and kiss her. On her broad mouth. On her soft hard full lips.

'Are you sure?' she is breathing the words right into my mouth.

I hesitate for a second because I don't know where this is going. Then suddenly it occurs to me that not knowing is good. All I do know is my travels, this is where they have brought me. I say to her: 'I am.'

Acknowledgments

'Late Fragment' from *All of Us: the collected poems of Raymond Carver*, published by Harvill Press. Copyright © Tess Gallagher. Reprinted by permission of The Random House Group Ltd.

'The Cinnamon Peeler' by Michael Ondaatje, *The Cinnamon Peeler*. Picador, 1989. Copyright © Michael Ondaatje.

'California' by Joni Mitchell, *Blue*, Reprise Records, 1971. Copyright © Joni Mitchell.

Every effort has been made to contact the copyright holders of material in this book. However where an omission has occurred, the author and publisher will gladly include acknowledgment in any future editions.

Thanks to my agent Jenny Darling for support, editorial feedback, friendship, and, for a few months there, some office space. Thanks to my publishers at Text Publishing,

Patty Brown and Michael Heyward. Thanks to Amanda Brett, for jokes and editing.

For a cover and friendship, thanks to Chong Weng-Ho.

Thanks also to my dear friends and colleagues who endured endless conversations about, and gave much needed feedback on, *Geography*, most particularly Tony Ayres, Kate Cole-Adams, Emily O'Connell, Jane Gleeson-White, Greg Hunt, Daniel Joyce, Kim Langley, Christine McMahon, Helen Murdoch, Meredith Rose and Leigh Small. Thanks too to all of the writers I have worked with over the years who allowed me to edit them, and talk about the writing process.

For help with obscure (well, obscure to me) facts, thanks to James Button, Saul Cunningham, Gideon Haigh, Adrienne Nicotra and Matthew Stephens.

For providing a place to write, thanks to Peter Bishop and Inez Brewer, and the Varuna Writers' Centre.

And finally I would like to thank Virginia Murdoch for many, many things—including her editorial work and IT know-how.

3
A modern-day *Story of O*
Julie Hilden

Maya and Ilan have an unusual marriage: Maya agrees to tolerate Ilan's chronic infidelity as long as she can participate and he will never stray without her. To her surprise, she finds their threesomes as arousing as they are disturbing, and for a while, everything seems fine. But as Maya's writing career takes off and she becomes more independent, Ilan feels threatened, and opts for another kind of sexual experimentation – one that plays on Maya's fear and ultimately threatens her life.

A compelling chronicle of obsession and power, *3* brings new immediacy to a timeless question: What is the greatest sacrifice you would make for love?

'IN THIS TERRIFIC DEBUT, JULIE HILDEN DOES WHAT FEW WRITERS CAN OR DARE TO: SHE HAS WRITTEN AN EROTIC, TRULY SEXY THRILLER. *3* IS SMART, SEXY, STRANGE, AND IMPOSSIBLE TO PUT DOWN'
Dan Shapiro, author of *Family History*

0 552 77177 5

BLACK SWAN

LONG GONE ANYBODY
Susannah Waters

Where do people go when they disappear?

That boy you went to school with, the girl who shared
your university room for a term, the neighbour you
glimpsed through the curtains – where did they go
when they left?

A nineteen-year old runs away from her life and
keeps on running. Haunted by the unexplained
departure of her mother four years earlier, she is
looking and not looking. Adopting one identity after
another – female escort, apple-picker, cashier, canvas
girl in a travelling circus – she is afraid to slow down
for fear of what, or who, may catch up with her. When
anonymous postcards start to arrive at every place she
goes, she is finally forced to confront the fate of her
long-gone mother? Can this runaway-girl escape the
same end?

In a compulsive and moving novel riddled with
family secrets, a predictably happy ending is never a
guarantee. But one thing becomes certain; people can
only ever save themselves.

0 552 77221 6

BLACK SWAN

SUBMISSION
Marthe Blau

You'll want to scream, but you'll be gagged.
You'll want to cry, but you'll be blindfolded.
You'll want to run away, but you'll be tied up.
You'll have no way of begging me, I'll do what I want
with you.

A story of sexual obsession, domination and extreme desire, *Submission* tells of a young married Parisian lawyer swept up in a cycle of sado-masochistic lust. A handsome stranger she meets in the courts issues her with a series of instructions which she finds herself compelled to follow. As the violence of their encounters escalates, these acts will become a dangerous addiction that she can't break. But how far can she go and how much of her life will she risk in the process?

Based on the author's own story, *Submission* sent shockwaves through the French establishment.

'THE BOOK'S CANDOUR RIVALS THAT OF *LA VIE SEXUELLE DE CATHERINE M*'
Sunday Times

0 552 77237 2

CORGI BOOKS

A SELECTED LIST OF FINE WRITING
AVAILABLE FROM CORGI AND BLACK SWAN

99946 6	THE ANATOMIST	Federico Andahazi	£6.99
77105 8	NOT THE END OF THE WORLD	Kate Atkinson	£6.99
99860 5	IDIOGLOSSIA	Eleanor Bailey	£6.99
77237 2	SUBMISSION	Marthe Blau	£6.99
77121 X	THE HOTTEST DAY OF THE YEAR	Brinda Charry	£6.99
99990 3	A CRYING SHAME	Renate Dorrestein	£6.99
99759 5	DOG DAYS, GLENN MILLER NIGHTS	Laurie Graham	£6.99
77080 9	FINDING HELEN	Colin Greenland	£6.99
77177 5	3	Julie Hilden	£6.99
77153 8	THINGS TO DO INDOORS	Sheena Joughin	£6.99
99807 9	MONTENEGRO	Starling Lawrence	£6.99
77190 2	A GIRL COULD STAND UP	Leslie Marshall	£6.99
99977 6	PERSONAL VELOCITY	Rebecca Miller	£6.99
77202 X	THE SOCIETY OF OTHERS	William Nicholson	£6.99
99536 3	IN THE PLACE OF FALLEN LEAVES	Tim Pears	£6.99
77106 6	LITTLE INDISCRETIONS	Carmen Posadas	£6.99
08930 3	STORY OF O	Pauline Reage	£6.99
77093 0	THE DARK BRIDE	Laura Restrepo	£6.99
77181 3	BETWEEN TWO RIVERS	Nicholas Rinaldi	£6.99
77145 7	GHOST HEART	Cecilia Samartin	£6.99
77166 X	A TIME OF ANGELS	Patricia Schonstein	£6.99
99864 8	A DESERT IN BOHEMIA	Jill Paton Walsh	£6.99
77221 6	LONG GONE ANYBODY	Susannah Waters	£6.99
77107 4	SPELLING MISSISSIPPI	Marnie Woodrow	£6.99